JOSEPH C

WORLD WITHOUT WANT

A
MARK HAZARD
THRILLER

EPIC PRESS

Published by:
Epic Press Ltd
PO Box 30108
Walnut Creek, CA 94598
josephcovinojr@gmail.com
First *Epic Press Ltd* Edition published 2022
Disclaimer:
*This is a work of fiction. Names, characters, places and inci-
dents either are products of the author's imagination or are
used fictitiously. Any resemblance to actual events or locales or
persons, living or dead, is entirely coincidental.*

DEDICATION

For
My Beloved Father
Joseph Covino, Sr.

In Honor
Of
The Memory
Of
The Late, Great
Sir Sean Connery,
The
Handsomest, Most Charismatic, and
Most Talented Cinematic Actor
Ever To Grace The Silver Screen,
and
Forever Filmdom's One and Only
True and Irreplaceable
James Bond 007

CONTENTS

PROLOGUE:

SAFETY OF THE REALM

RED SEA

Fast and Feared is her motto! Through the world's northernmost tropical sea, the sharply flared bow of the enormous guided missile destroyer sliced its way, cutting a smooth swath across its tepid and salty waters so renowned for their red–coloured sea sawdust. She was an all–steel, Kevlar–amoured, superstructure of the USS *Arleigh Burke*–class, her 505–foot long hull propelled through the biblical **Sea of Reeds** by gas turbine–driven, twin–shafted, five–bladed, reversible, controllable–pitch propellers—her cruising speed in excess of thirty knots! Her advanced Mark 41 vertical launching system(VLS)prepared to launch Tomahawk Land Attack Missile(TLAM)s, pre–loaded into pressurized canisters— or launch tubes—from its rows of multi–cell modules below the ship's deck.

A red, white–lettered sign cautioned:

DANGER. STAND CLEAR OF LAUNCHER DECK AREA.

A mannish voice from Fleet Control made the sedate announcement three times:

"Imminent launch. Imminent launch. Imminent launch. Sixty seconds. Stand by to launch."

Presently, the final countdown commenced:

"Ten–Nine–Eight–Seven–Six–Five–Four–Three–Two– One—Launch!"

Erupting violently with a fiery, orange outburst—the module's uptake hatch flying open—the long–range, jet–powered, subsonic cruise missile burst explosively out of its cell! It was a BGM–109 Tomahawk, carrying a thousand–pound, W80 cluster warhead. Trailing its arched, billowing pillar of gray smoke, the elongated, 3500–pound, 21–foot missile blasted off—sky–rocketing to its destination in excess of 550 miles per hour!

Hovering low over the faraway horizon was the big, blazing ball of the rising dawn sun. It was a perfectly serene morning for raining down death and destruction upon a defenseless and unsuspecting target!

§

PERSIAN GULF

Plowing through the tepid waters of the Persian Gulf, at the same time, was the Type 45 guided missile destroyer of the *D* or *Daring* class commissioned by the United Kingdom's Royal Navy. Her 500–foot hull was likewise WR–21 gas turbine–driven by twin–shaft, controllable pitch propellers. She cruised easily in excess of 32 knots—even though her power was decreased considerably when operating in the hot climate of what the ancient Assyrians called the Bitter Sea—otherwise known, most contentiously, as the Arabian Gulf.

"The American strike against Syria is now underway," the command centre's voice announced sedately.

Deep inside the destroyer's dimly lit operations room, the ship's nerve centre, crowded with manned computer consoles, the American launch was being monitored—closely tracking the missile's trajectory.

"Missile is launched."

"Full missile track."

"Target acquired."

"Closing."

"Missile's course is changing."

"Repeat"

"Missile's course is changing."

"Missile's course is being re–directed."

"Repeat"

"Missile's course is being re–directed."

"Missile's course has a new bearing."
"Repeat."
"Missile's course has a new bearing."
"Missile's new course heading is Turkish airspace!"
"Repeat."
"Missile's new course heading is Turkish airspace!"

§

Gölcük Naval Base
Gölcük, Kocaeli
Turkey

Gölcük Naval Base and Naval Shipyard, the Turkish Navy's main base, sprawl expansively along the east coast of the small inland Sea of Marmara, or Marmara Sea for short. Its various facilities spread over 1800 acres of land. Its namesake Marmara Island boasts a rich saturation of marble.

Pulling up to the checkpoint station emblazoned with the white–star–and–crescent Turkish flag, the sleek, black Etox Zafer sports car—powered by its 3.0–liter V6 engine—braked to an abrupt stop. Imprinted in the canopy overhead against the white plate were the blue letters:
ARAC GIRIS
(VEHICLE ENTRY)
A red signpost lettered in white read:
DUR KONTROL
(STOP CONTROL)
Steering the car was a burly Turk wearing the naval uniform of Regiment Commander for whom the square red flag–with–middle anchor would be flown.

In the passenger side sat a comely and dark young Trinidadian woman, her soulful brown eyes, set beneath thin brows, fixed straight ahead. Just beneath the right nostril of her delicate nose, a conspicuous beauty mark spotted her face. Her full, luscious lips parted slightly with a knowing smile, exposing gleaming white teeth.

His own lips pursed with an equally knowing smile, the Turkish Commander pondered the irony of his most immediate prospect. In Turkish the word, *Zafer*—the name of his sports car—means *Victory*: but he had a conquest of quite a different kind on his mind!

Receiving its clearance, the black sports car sped directly to the bleak building fronted by the tall, black, spiked iron gate and fence. Against the white awning above, a large blue plaque lettered in gold read:

GÖLCÜK MERKEZ KUMUTANLIGI
(GÖLCÜK CENTRAL COMMAND)

§

Once he securely locked himself and the young Trinidadian woman inside of his private Fleet Command office, the burly Turkish Commander yanked the gold window draperies forcefully snug. Then he turned to direct his lustful eyes to the girl, wearing a flimsy blue, tropical, ankle-length Maxi dress, and standing before him with a temptingly expectant expression on her face—her full and fleshy black bosom half–exposed and heaving. He licked his moist, openmouthed lips gluttonously. Then he bore down upon her, more like an attacker than a lover.

Grabbing the girl roughly by both of her bare arms, he smashed his mouth against hers with a reeking, vicious kiss. Her curvaceous breasts swelled against his barrel–shaped chest as she suddenly struggled to break free of his tenacious grip. He clung tightly to her wrists as she hammered at his chest with both of her clenched fists. Their feet scuffed awkwardly across the the flat, tapestry–woven, colour–threaded kilim rug spread over the polished wooden floor. Rashly, he tugged and tore off the thin straps of her top's plunging neckline. She unflinchingly backed away from him, clutching at her bared bosom.

"You're conveniently forgetting what you promised me for bringing you here!" he hissed at her through his gritted teeth.

"You're getting *nothing* from me!" she snarled, her tone defiant.

"We'll see about that!" he retorted, his manner becoming menacing. "Willing or not, I'll have *all* of you!"

"You'll be *dead* before you have *anything* of me!" she told him with a decided hostility.

Unbeknownst to him, her bitterly pronounced conviction was far more portentious—and preordained—than he could ever plausibly conceive!

Just then, that 21–foot, 1.5–ton, destroyer–launched Tomahawk missile was cruising toward its intended target at high subsonic speed! Guided over its evasive route by its inertial navigation system—with terrain contour matching—its rocket–propelled turbojet engine catapulted it over its preset course at 500 miles per hour! Its unfolded wings and fins completely spread, it flew low but full–tilt for making its precision strike!

Clutching at her soft throat with one hand, the burly Turk grasped one of her bared breasts with the other, groping hard as he shoved her forcibly backwards—slamming her into a dark maroon leather couch! Squirming, she struggled strenuously, her thickset thighs protruding from the slits of her split–leg gossamer dress! Clumsily, the Turk fumbled between her legs to tug at her nonexistent panties!

"What the hell's this?" he asked, aghast at touching the rigid boning of the stiff, spiral steel support garment she was wearing underneath her dress. "A Chastity belt?"

"It's a *corset*, you fucking moron!" she snapped.

Before the Turk could recover from his momentary shock and surprise—and react—the girl took him unawares: grasping at his ears with both hands and drawing him abruptly forward—biting savagely into his cheek with a gnawing tenacity!

"Get off me, you Turkish pig!" she seethed, quivering with rage as she kicked him backwards, both of her upraised feet flying!

"You black bitch!" the burly Turk muttered threateningly as he stumbled to his feet, groaning in pain and smearing blood from the deep gash in his cheek. "You're a dead woman!"

"We're both dead," she said serenely, stopping him in his tracks. "But I will die a *shahida* with my place promised in Paradise!"

"Allah Akbar! Allah Akbar!" she chanted calmly with upraised hands, repeating, "God is great! God is great!

In the same instant, that incoming Tomahawk missile delivered its deadly conventional warhead—detonating, in a flash, a thousand pounds of high explosives! And neither the burly Turk, nor the comely girl, ever really knew what hit them as the Turkish Fleet Command building violently exploded, blowing up in a convulsive, volcanic–like eruption of billowing, black smoke and flying structural debris!

§

KINGSTON, JAMAICA

Mark Hazard looked out on Kingston Harbour's gently rippling waters, shimmering with spangles of reflected sunlight. Clumps of darksome clouds hovered over the faraway horizon, aglow with the lustre of a pinkish sky—like the pink–decorated bedroom nearby. From the spare room in Mary Goodknight's little villa where he was lounging, he commanded a view of the world's seventh largest natural harbour; nearly landlocked and nearly ten miles long. A strong, cool breeze wafted throughout.

It was, indeed, a room with a view. And even though he'd shared the villa's only bath—and other intimacies—the view, or darling Mary's love for him, had yet to pall.

Suddenly, Mary's bare arms, scented with the garden flower fragrance of *Chanel No. 5*, snaked around his neck as she bent to softly kiss the corner of his mouth. Her bell of golden hair tumbled down to brush his face. He reached up, laying firm hold of her arms. Lifting up her soft chin with one hand, he kissed her full on the mouth, her lips still half–parted.

"Oh, Mark," she said, breathless. "It's so wonderful having you here!"

"It's wonderful being here," he said, and meaning it. "Why didn't we ever think of doing this before? Three years with only an office between us? What were we thinking?"

"We weren't thinking. Or, if we were, we weren't sharing."

"Well, we're sharing now. So let's go and have some dessert."

"Dessert?" Her wide–apart blue eyes expressed her puzzlement.

"After we've had dinner, I mean," he teased with a soft pat to her tender bottom. "Or rather, after I've had *you* for dinner!"

"For heaven's sake, Mark! Must you always be such a cad?"

"Always," he answered, reaching up to grasp her soft, rosy cheeks with both hands, drawing near to kiss her again— this time much more deeply than before.

§

MONA DAM RESERVOIR

Mark Hazard and Mary Goodknight strolled leisurely together, arm in arm, along the sandy footpath that sidled the reservoir's narrow roadway. They were making the round of the 1.6–mile loop that encircled some 700 million gallons of dull blue water, spreading far and wide before them, reflecting the clusters of darksome clouds hovering aloft. Across the reservoir, a long way off, the somber Long Mountain bulged from the facing shore. They were gradually approaching the northeastern section of their circuit. Mary dressed up for the occasion in her tight beige skirt and white tussore shirt.

"Why did you bring us here?" she asked him finally.

"Oh," Hazard brooded, "to pay my respects—and be with you."

"Respects?"

They paused at a gaping breach in the earthen embankment, rising some thirty–five feet, surrounding the reservoir.

"On an earlier mission of mine," he explained coldly, "two of my colleagues were murdered by the opposition and *disposed of* in this reservoir."

"I'm sorry."

Hazard shrugged slightly.

"It was a long time ago," he mused. "Long before you ever became my...*secretary*."

"Now I'm cooking for you and ready to sew your buttons back on if need be," she said demurely, looking down her dainty nose at him.

"Pretty treacherous and lethal conduct in these feminist times," he remarked.

"I would do much more," she said, unhesitating.

"You're a treasure," he told her, "you could tempt a man to resign."

"Resign from what?"

"This ghastly business we're in."

"Are you sure you wouldn't want to sleep on that?"

"We've slept on it quite enough, I should think," he said coyly. "And you're a girl to have around always."

Startlingly, out of the blue, the black, lightweight, twin-engine **AgustaWestland AW109** helicopter—its turboshaft powerplants driving its fully articulated four–blade rotor system—loomed ahead, decelerating as it descended to slowly lower its elegantly designed fuselage until it hovered over a spacious expanse of grass. There it pitched slightly, its rotor arms swinging languidly, and settled with a light bump.

The two watched with wonder, warmly embraced, grimacing against the swirling dirt and sand blown up by the machine's roaring engine. They stood, spellbound, as the cabin's door flew open and a tall, lanky figure in gray alighted to the ground. He was a gaunt man with strangely angular features, wearing a heavy–duty, double–breasted, gabardine Trench coat right out of the Cold War era! Leisurely, he moved toward them, both of his hands tucked deeply into his unbuttoned pockets.

Slowly stepping to the fore, Hazard positioned Mary Goodknight protectively behind his back as the stranger drew near. As the stranger came at them, Hazard abruptly produced his concealed **Beretta 70**, magazine–fed, single–action, semi–automatic pistol, leveling it at his hip!

"That's far enough," Hazard cautioned him with a grim smile.

"You're back to carrying a lady's handgun, I see," remarked the stranger, stopping dead in his tracks.

"You'll do for a lady—so it should work perfectly fine."

"Droll."

"What else are you? Besides a lady, I mean."

"Tallon," he introduced himself. "Ministry of Defence."

"Show me—slowly—by the fingertips."

Gingerly, the stranger drew both hands out of his pockets, peeling back the wide lapel of his coat with the fingertips of one hand, reaching in to pluck out his identification wallet with the fingertips of the other.

"Arm's–length," Hazard ordered tersely.

He held it out, a perturbed expression on his face.

Hazard stepped up sideways, abruptly snatching the brown leather case from the stranger's tenuous grasp.

"Stand still and keep those hands up," Hazard demanded, steadying his aim as he moved off to glance briefly at the plastic see–through compartment displaying its photo ID. "Well, there's no mistaking that eagle beak."

"You're rather edgy, Commander Hazard," the stranger remarked, looking scornfully down his aquiline nose.

"Spooks like you make me that way."

"Here!" Hazard added, stepping up abruptly to slap the wallet against the stranger's chest for him to clutch clumsily. "Now move over to the embankment."

"Really, Commander," the stranger protested, "this is becoming intolerable."

"Pity that. *Move!*"

At the earthen embankment, keeping his distance, Hazard prodded the stranger with a slight gesture of his pistol barrel.

"This is ridiculous," the stranger complained, "pintle–mounted machine guns are being trained on us as we speak."

"That's why I'm keeping *you* between us and them."

Mary Goodknight discreetly kept pace with them.

"Hands against the wall," Hazard directed the stranger, "feet spread apart. You know the drill."

"Outrageous," muttered the stranger as he grudgingly assumed the standard frisk position.

Hazard nuzzled his pistol snugly into the base of the stranger's spine. After running his expert hands deftly down his arms to the wrists, down his sides, down his backside, and down the insides of his thighs, he finally moved back from him.

"What do you want then?"

"You're to be flown to London straightaway," the stranger named Tallon announced testily, shaking himself as he stood up, erect but ruffled. "On Mr. EM's direct orders! A matter of state security and of the utmost urgency!"

"Is that so?" Hazard hissed.

"That is so."

Hazard re–holstered his gun in his chamois leather shoulder holster and harness.

"Stand there and wait."

Hazard turned to face Mary Goodknight.

"It looks like the VIP bus has come to collect me," he told her, caressing her arms consolingly. "Man's work, I'm afraid, darling."

"Overgrown school boys playing Red Indians, more like!" Mary scoffed.

"Pretty much the same thing."

"You were given three weeks' convalescence after that last Japan job!" she cried. "Damn you, Mark! Damn you all!"

"I know," he quipped, trying to placate her, "and just as we were all set to defy polite society by breaking all those rules of propriety."

"What rules?"

"Sharing the same house without a chaperone—unmarried—remember?"

"You will take care, won't you?" she said, ignoring his jest, her eyes glistening.

"Oh, I'll do that, all right," he heartened her. "Now, be a good girl and keep my spare room open. So long, Mary, just stay out of trouble till I get back."

"You do that yourself," she said, her eyes welling out.

"Time *is* of the essence, Commander," Tallon intruded.

"Stuff it!" Hazard said, sedately, without ever taking his eyes off Mary as he warmly grasped her face in his hands. "The safety of the realm can bloody well wait for just this minute!"

He bent to kiss her quivering, half–parted lips ever so tenderly. Then, without a word, he turned on his heel to abruptly march off.

"Good luck!" Mary called out after him, her fingertips touching her mouth to keep his kiss there.

"We're off then!" Mark Hazard snapped at Tallon, adding scurrilously. *"Lady!"*

Then he strode grimly toward that parked helicopter, waiting so stoically, so indifferently, for him to embark— with Tallon hurrying, but struggling, to catch up.

ONE:
LICENCE TO LIQUIDATE

M ark Hazard rode the lift up to the building's topmost floor, the eighth. It was inside that tall, grey building near London's Regents Park. He was the senior member of the Zero–Zero Section of the Secret Service. He strode along the quiet, thick–carpeted corridor to the leftward, green baize door that opened up to the offices of Mr. EM—Executive Minister of the Secret Service—and his attractive, all–powerful, private secretary, Miss Manypenny.

Manypenny was seated at her computer console, wearing a blue–and–white stripe shirt with a plain, dark blue skirt. She lifted up her soft brown eyes to meet Hazard's blue–greys with her warm and welcoming smile.

"You should go right in," she told him.

"Not time enough for even a late afternoon tryst?" he said suggestively, stooping to gaze desirously at her before carefully clarifying himself. "With my own secretary, of course."

"Not even in your most over–ambitious dreams!" she said, shaking her head playfully as she rested her chin on one hand, already pressing the intercom button with the other. "Zero–Zero Eight is here, sir."

"Send him in!" came the gruff response, the voice metallic.

Hazard straightened himself with a shrug of his shoulders, widening his eyes worriedly. Then he shouldered his way through the double, red–padded doors—above which the circle of light blinked from red to green for private conference!

Hazard stepped inside Mr. EM's plush office, setting foot on the thick green carpet, pulling the door quietly shut behind him.

"Good afternoon, sir."

EM was standing at the window, its venetian blinds raised, looking out on the sprawling, 410–acre park, the treetops of its inner and outer ring roads spreading right and left far off below.

"The only trysting you're going to be doing," he said testily, glancing around at Hazard, his cold, grey eyes reproachful, "is on a flight to Syria!"

"Sir," said Hazard, abashed. He stood almost at attention, hands clasped behind his back, awaiting EM's bidding.

Tamping his pipe's tobacco, EM struck a match to ignite it, taking tugs at the stem to get it going.

"Sit down, Zero–Zero Eight," he told him.

"Thank you, sir."

Hazard sat down in the sole chair placed in front of the broad, red leather–topped desk lit up by a spangle of yellow light shed by a glass, green–shaded reading lamp.

"I tell you, Mark," EM said pensively, heaving a heavy sigh of smoke, "it's a world gone mad out there."

"Sir?" Hazard said lowly, his eyebrows raised by EM's unexpected utterance of his Christian name, not to mention his sudden change in tone.

"I'm here to be of service, sir," said Hazard assuredly, facing and staring straight ahead at the wall opposite.

"I know you are! I know you will be!"

Agitated, EM moved behind his desk, tapping the smooth, briar bowl of his bent Billiard upon its leather top before tossing it aside altogether, disgustedly.

"It's this nasty, neverending Islamic State business!" EM declared finally as he slid heavily into his tall–armed, polished blue leather chair, his weathered face and iron–gray hair illuminated by the desk lamp.

"Terrorists, sir?"

"Or Liberators—depending upon whose propaganda you subscribe to."

"Sometimes though," EM went on, giving voice to some rarely expressed private sentiments, "I wish to God that we would just get out of these damned Mideastern countries and leave them to their own devices—and their bloody oil!

Centuries of fractious empire–building has bought us far more enemies than friends—yet we still haven't learnt the lesson!"

"I'm no historian, sir," Hazard offered, "but I suppose that Britain's left her mark in plenty of positive respects."

"No doubt! Great Britain's grandiose legacy is all but guaranteed. That's all academic. What's a lot trickier to deal with is the pushback by these countries ready and willing to resort to whatever means to resist—and defeat—the hegemonic designs other nations have on them."

"Terroristic means."

"Precisely."

"Sir," Hazard ventured hesitantly, "the Islamic State's not a country as such."

"Goes without saying," EM conceded with a decided nod. "They're far, far worse—it's a bloody, violent *network* with its tentacles reaching all the world over. A super–terrorist security apparatus with death squads and secret police gangs. Its supporters and sympathizers, too—collaborators in every quarter of the globe—hundreds of British citizens right here in the United Kingdom no less! There never would have been any damned Islamic State were it not for that ill–advised invasion of Iraq by the Americans!"

"Most members of its security forces being former military and intelligence officers from Saddam Hussein's Arab Socialist Ba'ath Party, or so I gather from our own reports."

"That asinine action single–handedly spawned this entire militant Islamist group."

"What's our problem then, sir?"

"The slippery nature of this enemy," answered EM with a dismissive wave of his hand. "Their sheer elusiveness as an adversary. As you know, Britain's allied with the United States coalition spearheading the military campaign against the Islamic State, mostly via indiscriminate airstrikes—the Combined Joint Task Force."

"Operation Inherent Resolve?" Hazard recalled.

"Operation Inherent *Insanity!*" EM spouted irately much to Hazard's unexpected dismay. "More like!"

"Sir?"

"Tens of thousands of sorties flown to date with un-counted thousands of civilian casualties exterminated in the process with no letup in sight—our own Royal Air Force carrying on roughly a third of those!"

"Collateral damage being the *im*polite euphemism, I gather, sir."

"Quite," EM added indignantly. "The Americans remain under the misguided impression that they can simply bomb this volatile enemy into oblivion—or at least slaughter untold thousands trying! Sheer lunacy, I tell you!"

"Where does our department come in to all of this?" Hazard asked, slightly impatient.

"Are you fit?" EM asked without warning.

"As fit as can be," Hazard equivocated, "I suppose, sir. Why?"

"Because," EM said irritably, "what I detest the most about this whole sorry affair is being forced to send one of my best agents into harm's way on some lunatic mission—against probably the most dangerous opposition he's ever had to confront!"

"All in the line of duty, sir."

"Laudable sentiment," EM affirmed, "but you're going to need a lot more than plucky heroics to get you through this assignment unscathed. This isn't your line of country, I assure you!"

"I'm in pretty good shape, sir."

"You'll need to be. This is a tough one. And you'll need to be able to take care of yourself."

"I should be all right, sir."

"Make no mistake about this assignment then," EM be-labored the point. "There are plenty of treacherous people you've never met, and some of them might be mixed up with this business. Some of the most insidious. So I've thought twice before involving you in it."

"I'm still keen to have a go, sir."

"Good. Let's get on then."

"It's been demonstrated," EM continued to relate gravely, "that somebody, somewhere, has developed a super sophisticated homing device—capable of not only deflecting a missile in flight, diverting it from its course, but also redirecting, or rerouting it toward a different target entirely! How—or for what ultimate purpose—we don't know yet.

"Our Type 45 air–defence destroyer, HMS Daring, was deployed to the Persian Gulf to assist in Operation Inherent Resolve. She was monitoring the Tomahawk missiles fired against targets in Syria by the American guided missile destroyer, the USS Arleigh Burke, whilst deployed in the Red Sea. One of those first missiles was deflected, and re–directed, to destroy the Fleet Command building at Turkey's Gölcük Naval Base!"

"I take it there's a connection with this incident to the Islamic State," Hazard surmised.

"You take it correctly," EM said.

"From my briefings on the Islamic State, though, I shouldn't have thought that they're really capable of that kind of technical sophistication in their weaponry."

"That's precisely what you're being sent to Syria to find out—if they are or aren't—and, if not, then who is and why!"

"What's the link to Syria, sir?"

"That's the one curious anomaly occurring, coincidentally, at the time of the missile strike against the Turkish Fleet Command building."

"And that is, sir?"

"Minutes preceding the missile strike," EM recounted, "a high–ranking Turkish Fleet Commander brought on base a young Trinidadian woman—caught on security cameras at the vehicle checkpoint."

"Presumably," Hazard remarked knowingly, "this mysterious lady's been duly identified?"

"Indeed, she has," EM confirmed, "by MİT, the Turkish state's National Intelligence Organization."

"Is she someone significant?"

"Her name was Gayla Soo. She was a so–called Bride of the Islamic State. She was a member of the all–woman Khansa Brigade."

"Said brigade being based in Raqqa, I presume."

"Correct."

"Am I to understand then, sir, that I'm to go undercover with an entire brigade of potentially beautiful and fanatical female terrorists?" Hazard quipped.

"Take this assignment lightly, Zero–Zero Eight," EM admonished him, "and the place you'll mostly likely wind up going undercover in will be a *body bag!* It's no laughing matter!"

"Sorry, sir."

"You're booked on a flight to Aleppo, where you'll connect with a train to Raqqa. In Raqqa, your contact will be an agent named, Yasin Salih. He'll orient you to the local situation. And see to it that you keep your appointment with the Armourer—he's put together a smart–looking suitcase for your trip. Well, that's all."

"Yes, sir," said Hazard, getting sturdily to his feet.

"Just remember this, Mark," EM reminded him solemnly. "carrying a Zero–Zero number means that you're Licenced to Liquidate—not to get liquidated. So whilst you're out in the field on this particular assignment, I trust that you'll be emboldened to liquidate the *hell* out of the opposition!"

TWO:
GOING BEHIND THE SUN

ALEPPO, SYRIA

Mark Hazard smiled wryly at his own reflection, mirrored in the stretch acrylic Plexiglas of his cabin window: his was a lean and hard–looking face with deeply–etched features, deep–clefted cheeks, and a strong, solid chin. A black lock of hair leafed over his right brow. His expressive eyes were wide but deep–set beneath bushy but dark and straight brows. His eyes were blue–grey, cold and arrogant, though they could quickly turn ironical, even whimsical. His nose was straight and sturdy, his mouth cruel and sensual, betraying a potentially brutal and ruthless nature that lay dormant, smoldering just beneath that remarkably cool exterior, just waiting to be provoked into action. His visage was aglow from the LED mood lighting shed by the passenger service unit component installed in the overhead panel.

Aleppo, Syria's second–largest city, is one of the oldest continuously inhabited cities in the world. It sprawls upon a plateau 1250 feet above sea level about 75 miles inland from the Mediterranean Sea. Spreading over more than 73 square miles, the city's surrounded to the north and the west by farmlands, cultivated extensively with olive and pistachio trees. To the east, the city approaches the parched, arid areas of the Syrian Desert—its 200,000 square miles of wide open, rocky, gravelly chert desert pavement of stony cobbles and pebbles, composing over half of the country!

More relevant to Hazard's purposes was the city being situated just 28 miles east of the international Syrian–Turkish border checkpoint—the **Bab al–Hawa Border Crossing**—or **Gate of the Winds Crossing!** Known for its lengthy lines of buses and trucks, it links the Syrian M45 and the Turkish D827 highways, and would make one hellacious escape route!

Hazard, however, was destined to see precious little of the city outside of Aleppo International Airport, which serves as a secondary hub for Syrian Arab Airlines, Syria's national flag carrier airline! And just then, Mark Hazard—secret agent for the British Secret Service—was a passenger on that SyrianAir flight out of Beirut bound for Aleppo!

Powered by two wing pylon–mounted IAE V2500 turbofan engines, the narrow–body, low–wing, single–aisle Airbus A320 aircraft was on its final approach to make touchdown at the airport. Once the twinjet airliner landed, its retractable tricycle landing gear gently setting down its 123–foot–long airframe onto the runway, Hazard caught his first glimpse of the modern, four–floor, terminal facility—a beige building that intermingled contemporary and Islamic architecture.

Customs Check Area

So read the emblazoned wall banner beneath its translation into cursive, Arabic script. Hazard went through the passport control check and waited for his suitcase to come off the jet.

A tall, shiny bald man with a paunchy midriff, wearing just rumpled dark trousers and a baby blue shirt, eyed him suspiciously, looking him up and down: his single–breasted suit in dark blue light–weight worsted, white nylon shirt with foulard tie, and hand–stitched black moccasin casuals.

Mark Hazard's painstakingly prepared passport and papers were all quite in order. His cover was a simple but credible one: he represented **Transworld Corporation** and was traveling to Raqqa to assist with continuing the work of the laudable Scanning for Syria project—scanning and digitalizing excavated clay tablets with cuneiform writing, creating moulded cast copies of archaeological objects endangered by the country's ongoing civil war. Start dissertating about 3D acquisition and printing technology together with X–ray micro–CT scanning, and your expedited passage through the customs is invariably well–assured!

Outside the customs, squares high up in the ceiling overhead threw down bright light upon the polished, shiny, checkered flooring below. Smart–looking traveling bag, indeed! It was instead a very battered, brown suitcase that Mark Hazard plunked down upon the blue vinyl seat amidst the hustle–and–bustle of the airport's crowded waiting area. It teemed with various indigenous Semitic inhabitants of the Eastern Mediterranean native to the Levant, Syrian Arabs and Palestinians mostly, Kurds, Turks, Armenians, and Assyrians included—a fascinating cross section, thought Hazard.

"Mr. Hazard?" came the stranger's hoarse voice from out of nowhere.

"Yes?" he whirled around to confront whoever was accosting him.

He was a somewhat short gentleman, elderly looking and grayheaded, aged beyond his fifty–ish years. His eyes were small and slanted, Hazard noticed, tired and bagged, weary from indescribable fatigue—or anguish.

"I'm Yasin Salih," he greeted Hazard with a broad, swollen smile. "I'll be your host and guide while you're in Syria. I thought that I should personally escort you to Raqqa to expedite your trip there."

He was wearing blue jeans and a baby blue sportshirt— much alike the customs official's. Hazard was wondering, rather satirically, whether it was some new national uniform.

"Our car's waiting outside," he said, gesturing with the arm draped with his folded brown leather jacket.

"Most considerate," said Hazard, picking up his suitcase and gesturing to Yasin Salih to lead the way out into the cool, semi–arid steppe air.

§

Yasin Salih showed Hazard the way to that iconic symbol

of travel, a parked, mustard yellow Mercedes–Benz W123, 240D model executive car taxicab, a four–door saloon. A stocky driver with close–cropped hair, narrow eyes, and a stubbly chin got out to load his suitcase into the boot.

"I'll do it," Hazard told him, raising a halting hand. Applying pressure with his other hand, a flat, side, lead–lined concealed compartment quietly slid open—delivering into his warm palm his loaded Beretta 70, magazine–fed, single–action semi–automatic pistol! Surreptitiously, he quickly tucked the handgun into his waistband.

As he slid into the back seat alongside Yasin Salih, Hazard just as calmly pulled out the pistol and leveled it at the venerable gentleman seated next to him.

"Tell your friend to keep both hands on the wheel and to keep quiet," Hazard coolly commanded him.

Yasin Salih directed his driver to do precisely as Hazard ordered.

"Now," Hazard started nonchalantly, "before we proceed further—and unless you want an extra navel—show me the one you've got."

"Really, Mr. Hazard," Yasin Salih scoffed with a derisive snicker as he deliberately rolled up the bottom of his shirt.

Presently exposed to view—stretched across Yasin Salih's midriff—were the firm and fibrous lesions that formed the overgrowth of rubbery, dark brown *keloid*, or *keloidal*, scar tissue. In Yasin Salih's case, such scarring was directly attributable to that *strike branding* method of human torture!

"Satisfied, Mr. Hazard?" Yasin Salih asked quizzically.

"Fair enough, Mr. Salih," Hazard answered, tucking away his handgun with an affirmative smile. "Let's get on then!"

§

ALEPPO RAILWAY STATION

Yasin Salih's driver steered the 4–speed automatic Mercedes–Benz, boasting its 72 PS metric horsepower, pulling
up to a stop outside of Aleppo's lofty and stony two–story
railway station, the city's main and second oldest. Its facade
was dimmed by the gentle glow of twilight. In its spacious
and splendid lobby, set in the middle of its shiny polished
floor, a spouting, octagon–shaped fountain of mosaic was
overhung by a glittering chandelier suspended from the ceiling. Curiously, a lone grandfather clock stood tall against
one wall. Passengers' voices echoed hollowly off the walls.

It was built as part of the Berlin–Baghdad railway, ulti-
mately reorganized as the *Chemins de fer syriens*, or CFS, the
national Syrian Railways operator headquartered in Aleppo.
Its network operations are designed entirely around diesel–
electric traction, the system possessing low level capacity—
with top track speeds ranging from roughly 50 to 75 miles
per hour.

Hazard and Salih were soon seated together in the air-
conditioned passenger coach of their shiny, silver, stream-
lined DMU–5 locomotive bound for Raqqa. They rested
their elbows on a slender, wooden table set between them
and their cushioned, high–backed chairs. Bowling along, the
train screeched slowly across the tracks.

"I got those scars in Tadmor Prison in Palmyra," Salih
related sedately. "I'm a graduate of prison."

"I'm sorry," Hazard condoled. "A notorious place, I've
heard."

"Notorious for its horrific cruelty. It's the absolute prison."

"Absolute?"

"Yes. It's just an enclosed place that doesn't open up except to dispense food—if you can call the rancid slop they
serve food—or punishment. In such a prison, time doesn't
pass, it accumulates over the prisoners until it suffocates
them. It's a place that literally eats men."

"Were there no basic rights, or privileges?"

"Rights? In Tadmor you have nothing. You're left with only fear and terror. It's been most aptly called a kingdom of death and madness. Torture was a daily ritual—a prolonged journey of pain and slow death. Death was a daily occurrence. As were non–stop executions, random beatings, eye–gouging, broken limbs, crushed fingers. Your life was worth nothing."

"It sounds more like a concentration camp than a prison."

"A concentration camp for torture, humiliation, hunger, and fear—one of the most vicious places on the planet. A *death* camp, really. Death stares you in the face at Tadmor, and is only avoided by sheer chance. You literally hang between life and death."

"Like living in hell itself."

"It's a hell of a very particular kind, my friend. I'm a returnee from that hell."

"You must have many terrible stories to tell."

"Too many, which is why I'm so reluctant to do so. I dislike talking about fear. And Tadmor was a symphony of fear—and terror—just torture and fear, morning, noon, and night. Fear was a way of life, where every day primitive and vengeful torture was carried out at the hands of heartless people. You feel you are at the end of the world. To tell it, you have to re–live the ordeal all over again."

"What drives a regime to commit such atrocities?"

"It's a thuggish mentality, Mr. Hazard. There's a saying in Syria, that if you do something wrong—which can simply mean being at the wrong place at the wrong time—you will *go behind the sun.*"

"What in hell does that mean?"

"It means, my dear friend," Salih said solemnly, "that you just—*disappear.* Mind, that doesn't befall you."

"I'll make a note to stay in front of the sun then."

Salih smirked at Hazard's ironical remark.

"Now," he suggested, changing the subject, "are you ready to hear the most shocking revelation?"

"I'm ready for most anything at this point, I think," Hazard said with a nod.

"The Islamic State recently destroyed Tadmor prison!" Salih related gravely.

"The Islamic State?" Hazard repeated, taken aback.

"The very same Islamist group that you've come to grapple with."

"How?"

"They blew it up! Completely demolished it! Reduced it to rubble! They detonated IEDs!"

"Improvised explosive devices? They're not demolition experts then?"

"They don't have to be—not as long as they're that efficient—and effective."

"Surely," Hazard thought out loud, sounding baffled, "what they did was a good thing!"

"It could be a propaganda ploy to recruit new militants to their group."

"Only, I was given to understand that they're the *villains!*"

"In Syria," Salih recounted, "the situation's incredibly complicated. It's a jungle in a state of savagery. It's difficult for anybody to tell who the real villains are anymore. Some say the repressive regime is the villain. Others say it's the radical rebels. That one or the other is the greater or lesser of two evils. Still others say it's interfering countries like yours that bomb Syria with indiscriminate airstrikes!"

"What do you say?"

"I'm just the humbled resident dissident, Mr. Hazard—too timid and soft–spoken to pose any threat to either side, though both sides would like to see me dead. It's a part that I play well to survive. Besides, after years of hiding among the Syrian underground, I was eventually caught—and served my time at Tadmor. Sixteen years, Mr. Hazard, sixteen years..." his melancholy voice trailing.

"Good God!" Hazard looked aghast, rubbing his dropped jaw.

"I think those who say Syria's sides are equally evil are the same people who believe in that despicable slogan of *Realpolitik*: a devil you know is better than a devil you don't know."

"Meaning the devil you know isn't really a devil after all," Hazard agreed knowingly.

"It's only the devil you don't know who is the villain," Salih concurred. "This is poor politics, devoid of knowledge, devoid of human values."

"Is there a devil involved in this mess whom we don't know?"

"There's a hundred and five miles to Raqqa to traverse," Salih told Hazard with his expressive smile. "So there's plenty of time to thrash it out and nominate our favorite suspects."

THREE:
WAITING
BY
THE
RIVER

Train sounds can be strangely tranquilizing. As their train hurtled toward their destination, the hasty metal clatter of the wheels, the metallic rattle of the couplings at either end of the car, the squeaky creak of the coach itself—all combined to lull both men into a soothing state of quiet calm.

"Tell me about this Khansa Brigade then," Hazard said, rubbing his drowsy eyes, struggling against the urge to just doze. "It's made up of all females, I gather."

"It's the morality police force of the Islamic State," Salih related with a slight yawn, "otherwise known as *Hisba*. It's an all–women battalion."

"Terrorists as morality enforcers," Hazard commented, "that's an interesting concept."

"Outsiders tend to associate acts of terror with men, presuming women to be inherently less violent. Yet, female insurgents have played integral roles in suicide bombings and other terrorist attacks throughout the Middle East. For its part, the Islamic State has actively sought to entice women into joining its ranks."

"In this setup," Hazard remarked, "their place is hardly in the home then."

"They're homemakers, right enough," Salih simpered contrarily, "just of a drastically different breed. You need to understand the background."

"I'm listening."

"This civil war in Syria is still ongoing," Salih recounted seriously, "and only recently has it scaled down. Once the Islamic State wrested full control of Raqqa, it made the city not only its chief command centre, but also its defacto capital. Residents in Raqqa call it *Al Tanzeem*—the *Organisation*. After interminable airstrikes by foreign powers, its fighters were forced underground."

"The men, you mean."

"Yes. The *women*...remain! Their enforcement unit op-

41

erates throughout the city, which is their stronghold. Like the male members of the Islamic State, the women of the Khansa Brigade are all armed."

"As combatants?"

"No. They don't participate in combat operations, but they are given weapons and weapons training."

"What is their function then?"

"They're tasked to patrol the streets of the city to enforce strict adherence to Sharia law. Their purpose is to maintain public *purity*."

"How do they set about doing that?"

"By making sure that any female in public is both fully covered and always accompanied by a male chaperone."

"Preferably a *respectable* male chaperone," Hazard sniggered.

"A *mahram*—a family member or relative."

"How do they deal with lawbreakers, pray tell."

"They punish them, of course—usually by flogging. They'll whip women with forty lashes merely for wearing makeup or high heels."

"Who qualifies for this vigilante brigade?"

"Young single girls—between the ages of 18 and 25— who speak Arabic. They're even allowed to drive."

"How very modern."

"As an extra incentive, they're paid a monthly salary of 25,000 Syrian pounds or lira! These women do not, however, commit conspicuous acts of terror that have made this extremist group infamous."

"But the jihadist movement has used women for years to carry out suicide jihadist attacks," Hazard observed.

"This brigade doesn't take part in terror operations," Salih said with a slight shake of his head. "But it does provide *recruits* for suicide missions."

"Now that's a mouth–watering morsel of intelligence," Hazard said approvingly.

"Are you ready to hear yet another startling revelation?"
"Try me."
"Most members who make up this brigade are Western women from English–speaking countries!"
"Foreigners?"
"Not just any foreigners, but *British* jihadist brides—they making up the majority!"
"You're joking!" Hazard exclaimed.
"Would that I were," Salih elucidated. "They could be ordered to carry out attacks on European soil. As women enjoy a positive security bias—being perceived as less threatening—they possess a greater potential for carrying out a successful attack."
"I see—" Hazard said blankly.
A lone, sullen young woman, profoundly fair of face—so to say per the nursery rhyme—seated nearby, her head and neck wrapped in a plain, white–cloth hajib, stared intently out the window, lost in thought. Her cheerless eyes glistened, reflecting the distress of some grievous heartache. Her deep contemplation arrested Hazard's attention.
With a lurch and a clang of the couplings, the train slackened speed. Hazard himself gazed through the window, pensive at first before turning very grave–faced, brooding upon the passing landscape. He suddenly commanded a panoramic view of the staggering scenery of war—and a ravaged city that lay in bombed–out ruins—a terrible tableau of battered and barren buildings; cavernous and crumbling structures of concrete and twisted and tortuous metal; heaping piles of crumbly rubble; moldering mounds of dirty and dusty debris. Hazard swallowed hard, choked by the ghastly sight of the shattered city spreading far and wide before him.
"You've never seen a city laid waste before?" Salih asked him, intruding upon his deep preoccupation with the grisly picture of widespread destruction. "Have you?"
"No," Hazard muttered absentmindedly, "I haven't. Nev-

er this close–up."

"Syria has been reduced to a battlefield of inhuman powers, Mr. Hazard," Salih told him solemnly. "And the American superpower has acted extremely inhumane towards my country. This course of events—these bombing raids—will lead to nothing. Air bombardments may damage the Islamic State, but they won't destroy it. It will keep its power to attack and even expand. It's not an army with heavy equipment, nor a state with a large infrastructure, which means that bombing it from the sky will have limited effect. The United States instigated this situation in which Syria would be plunged into chaos!"

"I'm sorry, Yasin," Hazard commiserated, "but I can't involve myself with politics."

"You may be forced to."

"What do you mean?"

"This is a sordid time—a time of sordid criminals," Salih maundered. "The freedom of my loved ones and the future of the world are interlinked. We have to tame the monsters of the world if we aspire to a less cruel future. We must tame the monster as much as we can to be able to survive it."

"Have you loved ones here?"

"I have a wife, Samira," Salih said spiritlessly. "She's a person full of humanity and love for people—one who lived among the people and struggled among the people. And this makes her a symbol of the character of the Syrian struggle."

"Lived?"

"Samira's a dissident like myself," he clarified. "She was abducted in Douma and is missing—and presumed murdered by Islamist militants."

"I'm truly sorry," Hazard desponded, hanging down his head but lifting up his sorrowful eyes with heartfelt pity for this man.

"At times," Salih told him, "especially after Samira's silent absence, I keep wondering if I have not been transformed into a monster myself. Does one really survive monstrosities?"

Hazard looked stupefied, speechless.

"There's a Chinese proverb," Salih went on, "that says if you wait by the river long enough, the bodies of your enemies will float by. The river of history is now controlled by our reckless enemies. They have done their best to own our change—to dispossess us from the ownership of our change and history. But in doing so they have unified our river with theirs—and their bodies will float soon in this one big river!"

"I'm at a loss...," Hazard said.

"It's the reality," Salih told him. "It's our situation. No life. No future. A world without alternatives. Nothing."

A shrill whistle blew long and loud. Slowing to a plodding speed—with a heavy sigh of vacuum brakes and a whistling whoosh of vented steam—the train ground to a fitful halt.

§

"Remarkable!" Hazard chuckled, lugging his suitcase, after Yasin Salih led the way on foot to a car repair shop near the train station, picking up a private car he'd left parked there.

"Several years ago," Salih related, "militants destroyed the train station via a VBIED—vehicle borne improved explosive device."

"Charming."

"I've been very remiss, my friend."

"Oh, how's that?"

"We've journeyed all this way and I've yet to offer you any refreshment. You must be famished."

"I could do with some savory Syrian cuisine," Hazard agreed as he loaded his battered brown suitcase into the car's back seat. "You can't go wrong with lamb, lentils—and Syrian beer."

"Good," Salih said with a nod. "I've already arranged for you to meet with a leader of the brigade at one of their *maqqars*."

"Maqqars?"

"All–female safe houses where single women live."

"Sounds like my kind of place."

"I wouldn't be too sure about that," Salih said contrarily. "These are dangerous women, my friend."

"All the more challenging."

"I pray you'll keep your good humor once you meet."

They got into the steel-gray Iran Khodro(IKCO)Dena— a front–wheel drive, four–door sedan named after the Dena peak in the Zagros Mountains in western Iran.

"This is an Iranian car!" Hazard said, surprised, sliding into the front passenger seat.

"With a modified Peugeot 405 platform," Salih affirmed, shifting behind the steering wheel, "but made in conjunction with SIAMCO—the Syrian–Iranian Automotive Manufacturing Company."

"Wonders never cease where economics is concerned."

"Quite."

§

Yasin Salih, an adroit driver, directly steered them to the outskirts of that terribly devastated city; prudently bypassing one of its numerous security checkpoints.

"By the way," Salih recounted to Hazard, "this brigade evolved out of security checkpoints."

"How so?"

"They were tasked with searching people who passed through checkpoints—partly to expose men who'd disguised themselves as women to avoid detention or recruitment."

"As *women?*"

"Or even enemy fighters, or infiltrators, hiding their identities behind the veil."

"That could be rather embarrassing for a soldier to be caught trying to sneak through in women's clothing."

"Practical—because men are forbidden from searching women themselves."

§

Route 4 was a narrow, two–lane road meandering through a flat and desolate wasteland. On the shimmering horizon, right ahead, there appeared a light–duty commercial vehicle painted cobalt blue. It was a rear–wheel drive, Hyundai Mighty truck. And it was barreling towards them at breakneck speed.

"Do you see that?" Hazard asked worriedly as he caught sight of the truck gradually crossing the road's median strip!

"I see it," Salih said, gripping the steering wheel tightly with both hands, knuckles bared.

By degrees, the screeching truck inched over the median as it bore down upon them, full–tilt!

"There's something you should know about militants in big trucks, Mr. Hazard," Salih suggested.

"What's that, Mr. Salih?"

"They love *ramming* things!"

"No need to play chicken with them," Hazard advised. "There's plenty of room to go off–road."

"Playing chicken is just what they're on about, I think!"

Just then, the speeding truck weaved back and forth across the median, careening heavily from side to side as it came at them! Salih started steering erratically, their Dena reeling to and fro!

"Go off–road now!" Hazard bellowed.

Salih wrenched the steering wheel hard to the right. Their Dena swerved sharply across the shoulder of the road, grinding to a screeching halt in a billowing cloud of desert dust as he applied the brakes! That oncoming truck screeched to a practiced stop, turned around in the middle of the road, and idled nearby.

Shaken from being forcibly thrown against the dashboard, Hazard let his passenger door hang open to fall out. He glanced around, squinting at Salih, who was bent forward, braced against the steering wheel—but budging. He suddenly sensed the powerful presence of strangers looming ahead and drawing near.

Before long, Hazard could focus and make out the trio of tall and dark figures hovering over them—three faceless, spectral shapes wrapped up from top to toe in long, flowing black robes and all brandishing Russian gas–operated, closed rotating bolt Kalashnikov assault rifles!

With all three of their 16.3–inch barrels—chambered for their 7.62x39mm rimless bottlenecked cartridges—leveled directly at them!

FOUR:
CREATING MEANING FROM MISERY

Surrounded by three brigade women, wearing full–length black niqabs and handily wielding their AK–47 assault rifles, Hazard and Salih surrendered to their custody.

"Follow me in the car!" their apparent leader ordered tersely, taking charge of Hazard's suitcase, returning with it to the long–cargo truck's double crew cab.

At gunpoint, Hazard and Salih were ordered back into their Dena—Salih behind the wheel, Hazard in the back seat.

"This is a *ladies* handgun!" the woman who frisked Hazard scoffed once she snatched his Beretta 70 pistol.

"So everybody keeps telling me," Hazard said with a grunt.

Presently, they were all on the road again with Salih steering the Dena—and following behind the Hyundai Mighty as it bowled along Route 4 once more.

"That wasn't a very ladylike thing to do," Hazard remarked finally, "running us off the road like that."

"Being ladylike isn't our purpose!" snapped the woman, leveling her rifle from the front seat.

"At the risk of making polite conversation," Hazard ventured, "what is your purpose?"

"We have established the brigade to raise awareness of our religion among women," she spouted devoutly, "and to punish women who do not abide by the law. Jihad is not a man–only duty. Women must do their part as well."

"How do you not abide by the law?"

"We arrest and punish women who do not follow the religion correctly."

"Sounds like a strict interpretation."

"That is why we are needed to raise awareness among women."

"Tell me," Hazard asked facetiously, "how long did it take you to memorize that bit of indoctrination?"

"Not as long as it takes to pull this trigger," she retorted with a low growl to her voice, "so don't tempt fate."

"You're a *strong* woman!" Hazard demurred, throwing up his hands in a display of mock capitulation. "I surrender a second time."

"Your so–called liberated woman—so full of corrupted ideas and shoddy–minded beliefs instead of religion—doesn't know what real strength is!" she exhorted him. "The model preferred by infidels in the West failed the minute that women were liberated from their cell in the house!"

"Model?"

"The *Western* model of women's emancipation—to leave her home to work—has failed!" she said, emphatic. "Women acquired nothing from the notion of equality with men except thorns!"

"Where is women's place then?"

"The fundamental function for women is in the house with her husband and children! Women have this heavenly secret of sedentary life—of stillness and stability."

"Under other circumstances," Hazard conciliated, "I could be inclined to agree with you. However, I have a slight quarrel with coercing compliance at the point of a gun."

"He's definitive proof of the rise in the number of emasculated men!" the woman seated next to Hazard, her gun accurately trained, finally spoke up.

"Perhaps we ought to put the *Biter* to use on him—on those most delicate of private parts!" her comrade jeered derisively.

They both cackled hysterically.

"What's the *Biter*," Hazard ventured, reluctant, "or dare I ask?"

"It's an instrument of compliance," related the brigade lady in front. "It resembles a steel–jawed animal trap with spiked teeth that clamp on the skin."

"A torture device?" Hazard sniggered.

"It would give new meaning to serving up your balls for breakfast!"

And again they cackled hysterically.

"Very funny," said Hazard, his brows raised quizzically, "but I could think of far better uses for them, thank you very much!"

"Like impregnating underaged virgins, no doubt!" she spouted bitterly, brandishing the barrel of her rifle at him. "That's enough out of you! It's forty–four miles to our destination. So just sit still and keep your filthy mouth shut!"

Yasin Salih listened nervously—but silently—to their uncommon conversation. And Hazard, for once, did exactly what he was told.

§

Qal'at Ja'bar
Lake Assad
Raqqa Governorate

A blazing, colossal, yellow ball, aglow against the fiery orange skyline, plummeted into that trackless, 240 square mile reservoir on the Euphrates River known as Lake Assad, Syria's sixth largest. It gave way later on to a luminous moon that shot its radiant beams across the breezy, rippling, blue waters washing the rock–bound left bank.

Arising from that jutting hilltop, converted into an is-land—its rock core surrounded by a dry moat—the lofty stone–built wall and ragged ruins of the **Qal'at Ja'bar** castle, together with its thirty–five bastions, hover high overlooking the Euphrates Valley. Its weatherbeaten, baked brickwork was crumbling all around. A winding, gravelly causeway led straight to its gatehouse and a roughhewn ramp carved out of rock. And the beamy headlights of the brigade's Hyundai Mighty and Yasin Salih's Dena threw swaths of bright light upon the crumbly baked bricks scattered all over.

53

"Carry it!" the brigade leader ordered Hazard, slinging his suitcase at his feet once they'd parked and stepped out of their vehicles.

"I'd handle that suitcase carefully if I were you," Hazard cautioned her, "it's booby–trapped, naturally."

"Carry it!" she repeated irritably, shining the bright beam of her torch in his face, making him wince.

"Yes, ma'am," said Hazard, snapping up his suitcase to tote.

They promptly fell in procession as the brigade leader led the way up a steep flight of dusty stone steps to the gaping, black mouth of a stony tunnel. Hazard and Salih followed on her heels. Those other two brigade ladies, their assault rifles carefully trained, brought up the rear. At the crest of those steps, their silhouettes crossed the threshold of the yawning gap in the rock. Then they climbed down a facing flight of stony steps that sloped downward, taking them deep into the castle's murky interior. They picked their way gingerly amidst the dusty rubble of baked bricks strewn all over the craggy floor—their unsteady footpath opening up to the crumbling remains of a vast, vaulted hall. At the foot of those steps, they came up to a dilapidated wooden door to some stony chamber.

"Put it down there!" ordered the brigade leader, flashing her torch at the base of the brick wall by the door.

"Yes, ma'am," said Hazard, plunking down the suitcase.

"Inside!" she ordered, opening up the creaking door that grated on its rusty hinges. "Both of you!"

Her two black–clad comrades stepped up to motion them to move with the barrels of their AK–47s.

"Yes, ma'am," said Hazard again as he and Salih obediently stepped inside the somber, cragged chamber with the wooden door slammed shut behind them.

"Woman of few words, isn't she?" Hazard remarked as they set foot on the dusty floor of the spacious, cragged room just dimly lit by the fitful flicker of a lone wall–torch.

"I'm afraid," Yasin Salih admitted forlornly.

"So am I—a little," Hazard said.

"I'm worried that this dismal place is our absolute last destination, my friend," he added, his tone ominous.

"We'll be all right," Hazard—even if doubtful himself—heartened him.

"From one prison into another," Salih said resignedly, throwing up his hands in a dejected gesture of defeat. "We've been crushed, it's true, but we create meaning from suffering."

"I'm sorry you're involved in this business."

They crouched together against the wall.

"My wife is my motivation to go on—and to go on deep in this desperate struggle for freedom."

"Samira?"

"The love of my life. Her absence is a big loss. My heart breaks every step of every day that I walk without her. Pain of this kind should not be suffered by any human being."

"And you really believe she would want you to endanger yourself like this?"

"She's a big element of my identity. I *am* Samira in her absence. I know that she wants me to keep on fighting. I will."

"She's never been seen or heard from since she was abducted?"

"I don't exclude the worst–case scenario about her fate, Mr. Hazard, but she's alive as long as the opposite is not proven. She's alive as long as I am living."

"I truly hope you'll be reunited with her somehow—someday."

"We struggle to the end, my friend. Hope needs us as much as we need it. Our powerful enemies don't feel safe and secure unless we surrender ourselves to despair. Despair is their friend, hope is ours."

"It seems there are so many enemies complicating this situation."

"At night, when I cannot sleep," Salih lamented, heaving a mournful sigh, "I struggle to understand what justice could possibly exist for those who snatch talented, brilliant people from their lovers' arms and leave us without answers."

"We're not alone," Hazard reassured him, "and we're by no means weak, so don't give up on justice just yet."

"The superpowers that've made life in Syria and the Middle East impossible are equally my enemies," Yasin Salih told Hazard solemnly, "but you are not one of them, my friend."

Salih held out his hand for him to take. Hazard pressed his hand, squeezing it tightly. Salih clasped their grip with his other hand, shaking it with a warm smile.

At that same instant, the three brigade women burst into the room, pointing their weapons toward the two men as they got hastily to their feet.

"Why have you come here?" the brigade leader asked abruptly, stepping up to confront Hazard.

"To extend our sincere condolences for the loss of Gayla Soo," he answered calmly, "for one thing. She was a martyr to the cause."

"What do you know of our cause, infidel?"

"The establishment of the worldwide caliphate, of course," Hazard proclaimed as convincingly as he could, "and the filling of the world with the truth and justice of Islam."

"How is this to be done?"

"By," Hazard stammered slightly, recalling their catechism, "putting an end to the falsehood and tyranny of unbelievers everywhere."

"Today," she declared wrathfully, "the soldiers of the Anti–Christ come every day and the hum of their jets can be heard as they come to throw bombs from the skies and demolish buildings, this is what the *ummah* faces!"

"*Ummah?*"

"Nation," Yasin interjected.

"The armies of the enemy," she ranted, "remain on its doorstep, working against its religion and trying to seize its resources and capabilities!"

"We sympathize," Hazard conciliated, "and we stand in solidarity in opposition to that."

"To *what?*"

"The hegemonic designs on the caliphate by the super-powers, of course."

"Are you a sympathizer or a spy?" she challenged him, drawing nearer.

"In fact," Hazard said dismissively, "we aspire to invest in your special project."

"What special project?" she asked him coyly.

"The enterprise involving certain high–tech equipment."

"I suppose you'd like to lay your hands on one of these as well?"

Slowly but surely, she reached into the rumpled folds of her black niqab and drew out a crumpled up woman's support garment—a laced *corset!*—and plunked it down on top of the lone, ramshackle wooden table set in the middle of the room.

"Well—yes," Hazard answered, clearly caught off guard, but brassing it out to the end.

"You're from Glasgow!" Hazard pressed her abruptly.

"What?"

"I know Glaswegian when I hear it!" he persisted. "My father was Scottish—from Glencoe!"

"Don't try and change the subject," she told him, indignant.

"Yes," the staid stranger's voice intruded unexpectedly, "don't try and change the subject."

His tall, dark, and slender silhouette darkening the door-way, the apparent soldier clad in camouflage combat fatigues stepped in the room, casually removing and pocketing his sunglasses. He had close–cropped hair, a dark mustache, and a stubbled chin. He looked robust, fit—and intelligent—his expression shrewd and discerning.

"I've heard enough," he said wearily. "This charade has gone on long enough."

He abruptly whipped out his Soviet Makarov PM semi–automatic, straight–blowback–action pistol that fired eight rounds of 9x18mm cartridges.

"Who are you working for and what do you want here?" he asked Hazard pointedly, aiming his pistol's 3.68–inch barrel straight at him.

"I'm working for Transworld Corporation," Hazard answered coolly, staring down his nose at the pistol's leveled gun barrel, "and we want the same thing you do—freedom from hegemonic tyranny."

"You sound like a poorly coached actor, my friend," the soldier sneered.

"I can prove it!" Hazard enthused, "I've brought a small donation as a token of our esteem—in my suitcase!"

"Bring his bag," he ordered the brigade lady guarding the chamber door, sounding irked.

Hazard took the suitcase, laid it down atop that table, and threw it open. It was closely packed with innocuous travel garments and accessories—including a large but flat navy blue, cardboard, two–piece garment box. After picking up the garment box and setting it down atop the table, separately, he hastily latched the suitcase shut and stood it up on end—deliberately positioning it so that he could stand, facing it from behind. He carefully slid it aside, making room for the garment box. Discarding its lid, he promptly broke open the garment box, exposing to view yet another carrying case altogether—a steel–gray, metallic briefcase!

"Carefully," the soldier cautioned him, "carefully."

His three brigade ladies pointed their weapons emphatically at Hazard, who gingerly picked up the metal briefcase and laid it open.

Its hinged halves leafed open, dividing into twin Acrylite compartments—numerous, neatly stacked bank notes showing through the left; an intricate, keypadded–and–wired explosive apparatus of rectangular, M112 demolition blocks, wrapped in olive Mylar–film containers surfaced with pressure–sensitive adhesive tape, showing through the right!

"There's a million dollars in bills," Hazard announced, "plus my insurance package: composition C–4 plastic explosive—with which, I'm sure, you're well familiar. Shall we talk business then?"

"A measly million dollars?" scoffed the soldier, laughing aloud. "You fool! The thing that we have can buy entire countries! With it we can conquer the world!"

"Don't waste your time, Mr. Hazard," Yasin Salih spoke up, interrupting them at last. "You can't bribe a nihilist Islamist militant any more than you can reason with a genocidal regime! They're both equally devoid of any kind of compassion! It's a disgrace that should shake every human being seeking a fair and just world, but—"

"Silence! You doddering old fool!" shouted the soldier, convulsed with rage.

Without warning, he stepped forward, took aim, and promptly fired his pistol—shooting Yasin Salih in the head and blowing his brains out!

FIVE:
COMRADE
TO
THE
RESCUE

Yasin Salih lay sprawled upon that brick–dust floor in a crumpled up heap, his obliterated head awash in pooling blood.

"You bloody bastard!" Hazard spouted through gritted teeth.

"Stand back and stand still!" ordered the soldier, taking hurried aim at his head.

"I came here in good faith," Hazard placated him, throwing up his hands in surrender. "I'm not an enemy!"

"Silence! You're a provocateur! And you're about to be executed as an enemy of the caliphate!"

"Stand there!" he ordered, turning on his heel as he gestured to the two nearest brigade ladies. "Watch him!"

Then he went over and through the chamber door, motioning to the brigade leader to go along with him. They left the door cracked ajar, standing just outside to talk together.

Nonchalantly, Hazard maneuvered himself behind his upright suitcase with the slightest steps in the dust.

"Stay still!" commanded the brigade lady nearest the cracked–open door, leveling her assault rifle at him. "Keep those hands where we can see them!"

"They're tired," Hazard grumbled with a slight sigh.

With a slight waving gesture, he started letting his hands down, lowering them ever so slowly until his open palms came to rest upon the innocuous sides of the suitcase.

"What are you doing?" she snapped.

"Just resting," Hazard said casually.

"Don't move!" ordered the brigade lady directly to his right as she deftly slung her assault rifle across her shoulder, whipping out his own Beretta 70 pistol to aim at him. "I think I might enjoy blasting you with your own little ladies gun!" she said scurrilously.

"I'm not moving," he assured her, his eyebrows raised quizzically. "I promise."

Hazard was banking on these two female fanatics being

somewhat visually impaired: the black niqabs which hung over their faces were made of *two* layers—a translucent layer and a second layer that covered any facial feature that might remain visible, even their eyes!

In each of the innocuous sides of his suitcase there was hidden a flat, stainless steel throwing knife forged by Wilkinson Sword, the British sword–maker! Hazard was an expert knife–thrower, too. Concealed cleverly by the rigid stitching at the corners were the tops of their handles. He pressed sideways. And just then, most stealthily, the steel handles of both knives slid smoothly into each of Hazard's palms! That deadly moment of truth had arrived!

"It's still a million dollars!" Hazard overheard the female brigade leader protest, raising her voice just outside of the cracked–open door.

"We're taking delivery of another device tonight at the Tabqa Dam!" the soldier retorted contrarily. "We don't need him or his pittance! Shoot the dog!"

That was it! Hazard's cue! He was left with no choice! To live—to survive—he had to act then and there! Without hesitation or pity! And his split–second timing had to be perfect—and unfaltering!

Hazard gripped both knives tight! In one convulsive, back–handed motion, he lunged sideways—thrusting it deeply into the nearest woman's breast until the ridge of his right hand felt fabric! At the very same instant—as synchronized as he could—the second knife flashed! And with deadly accuracy, he flung it across the room, plunging it deeply into the other woman's breast! Hazard's lips were compressed with unflinchingly grim determination.

In the very same faltering breath, both doomed women—paralyzed with pain and shock—let go of their guns, clutching at their breasts, protruding with those flat blades, tottering on their feet! They both retched hideously as they each started to keel over! For added measure, with a furious grimace on his face, Hazard reached out with his right hand, tightly grasping the nearest woman's veiled face before shoving her forcefully to the floor! His Beretta pistol dropped to the powdery brick–dust! He hustled headlong to snap it up!

Just then, the brigade leader burst into the room—hurriedly unshouldering her assault rifle to level and fire it! Taking quick but deadly accurate aim, Hazard cut her down with multiple, quickly squeezed–off rounds before she ever knew what hit her! He wasn't the best shot in Her Majesty's Secret Service for nothing!

Hazard crouched quickly behind that wooden table, taking careful aim across the top of it as he waited anxiously for that homicidal soldier to fall in behind her—only he never betrayed himself. Hazard overheard, instead, retreating footsteps scrambling across the crumbling baked bricks of that vast, vaulted hall outside. He was making a run for it, the bloody coward! His gun at the ready, Hazard slid warily to the frame of the open doorway to catch sight of the soldier's retreating silhouette heading for the exit tunnel's baked brick steps!

Hazard hurried back into the room, re–holstering his pistol. Between the leather and lining of his suitcase spine was packed—in two flat rows—fifty rounds of .32 ACP centerfire pistol cartridge ammunition. He coiled and crammed one row into each of his coat pockets. To hell with those assault rifles that he wasn't fitted for. He took one final hurtful look at Yasin Salih's supine shape before turning on his heel to go.

Then he snapped up his metal briefcase and chased after that murderous soldier! He drew out his gun again as he gingerly picked his way up and down those baked brick steps, following on the soldier's track, until he got to the outside—just in time to pick out the soldier taking off in a dark motorcar of his own! He opened up the door to Yasin Salih's Dena, tossing his briefcase and pistol onto the passenger seat, and jumped into the driver's seat! Igniting the engine, Hazard screeched off in a hazy cloud of dust in hot pursuit of the fleeing soldier!

§

Tabqa Dam
Raqqa Governorate

None of that strong–arm stuff, Mr. EM had reprimanded Hazard before sending him off on that damn Japan job, none of that gun–play he prided himself on so much. What in hell kind of mission was *this*—being forced to fight and kill young Mideastern *women*? This entire operation was outright...outrageous!

Hazard had no idea where he was going—or speeding to. All he knew for sure was that he desperately desired to kill the soldier who murdered Yasin Salih. So he gave chase for the express purpose of running him down and, most resolutely, doing just that. For roughly twelve miles, the narrow, winding roadway their two cars were racing across turned and twisted its way until there loomed ahead the uncommon contours of a singular structure, shooting up sky–high into the night.

Tabqa Dam, also known as Euphrates Dam, is a rolled earth–fill dam on the Euphrates river situated twenty–five miles upstream from the city of Raqqa. Syria's largest dam, it rises 200 feet and reaches 2.8 miles long. Rocky outcrops on either side of the Euphrates Valley, at the spot where the dam is located, stretch less than 3.1 miles apart. Situated on the southern end of the dam, its hydroelectric power station contains eight Kaplan propeller–type water turbines with adjustable blades.

Their two cars tore along the north–south roadway that stretched across the lofty crest of the dam from end to end. Hazard was gaining on the soldier and starting to overtake him when the most startling sight exposed itself to view:

a frightening roadblock of armoured personnel carriers, infantry fighting vehicles, self–propelled field artillery, and multiple rocket–launchers! And the soldier steered straight toward them—right into their open and welcoming arms; and armaments!

Recklessly, Hazard wrenched the steering wheel, swerved violently, and spun the Dena around in the middle of the roadway! From the opposite direction, out of nowhere, had materialized a similar array of military field artillery! And both battle lines were slowly advancing—and moving deliberately toward his position on the roadway! Christ! He'd landed smack dab in the middle of a bloody combat zone!

That reality hit home once the high–explosive 53–F–864 mortar projectile, containing 32 kilograms of explosive charge, detonated on contact as it blew up a blasted portion of the roadway—knocking Hazard off his feet as he fell out of the Dena! That mortar shell had been fired by a 2S4 Tyulpan—a Soviet 240mm self–propelled heavy mortar, carrying an externally mounted M–240 breech–loading mortar on the rear of the hull!

Hazard staggered over to a rust–colored metal railing sidling the roadway and stared down his nose at yet another startling sight: spreading far and wide before—and below—him were the gravity diversion Tabqa Dam's eight lengthy and steep concrete chute spillways—surging with frothy white water! There was absolutely no way out of that hopelessly impossible predicament except...*down!*

Glancing around, Hazard spotted a number of discarded and worn rubber car tires scattered, inexplicably, along the roadside. God knows why they were abandoned there! Keeping his wits about him, Hazard hurried back to the Dena, reaching into the passenger seat to grab his gun and break open his metallic briefcase! If he was going, he was taking out some of the bloody bastards with him! Punching the coded keypad, he quickly timed the briefcase bomb to detonate in just minutes!

Snapping up one of those rubber tires, Hazard mounted the metal railing, clambering over it. Feet–first, he sprawled prone upon a sloping flat baffle of smooth concrete block— one of several baffles separating the eight smooth declines slanting to the reservoir far off below. He clutched at the tire with outstretched arms. He started sliding himself down the sleek concrete baffle but the grade was just too damned steep! There was just no way that he could keep any traction at that near–sheer incline!

Helpless, Hazard slipped rapidly downward until he slid over the edge of the baffle and sailed into space! He plummeted just a short distance before plunging into the concrete chute of the gushing spillway itself! It took just seconds for him to be hurled headlong down the long, surging, sigmoidal–shaped spillway until he flew off the edge of its base, spilling over with the furiously rushing flow of water! Before he knew it, he was immersed in the chilly, cobalt blue, but surprisingly calm waters of the placid and expansive reservoir! He struggled to keep the tire upraised to stay afloat.

Those battle lines above, and afar, came to closer quarters but far too late to be impacted by Hazard's briefcase bomb once it went off and blew the Dena to bits—uselessly—leaving behind only the smoldering car's charred and burnt–out remains. Just as well, Hazard thought, as he vigorously shook his head to wring himself free of some of the wetness he was drenched with, released the tire—and started paddling toward the nearest low–lying, sidelong wall of the reservoir. After an arduous swim, once he was a long way off from the dam's spillways, he picked a spot to alight where gentle breakers rippled against the rock–bound shore. From that faraway vantage point, he watched intently the lofty crest of Tabqa Dam, ablaze with the firestorm ignited by the warring face–off of fighting regime and rebel forces battling and bombarding each other into oblivion. Mr. EM had indeed summarized it best: *madness!*

Out of a lurid, clear blue nocturnal sky, Hazard was taken aback once more by the most startling and unexpected sight: the **Mil Mi–8** medium, Soviet–designed twin–turbine helicopter suddenly—and ominously—hovering over him! This one was fitted out as an armed gunship. Its turboshaft engines reverberated deafeningly. Its whirling, sixty–nine–foot–ten–inch rotor blades were lowering towards him perilously close! His face smarted from being smitten by wind–whipped debris. He resigned himself that his end was near. Profoundly afraid, and fatigued, he reached into his left armpit and gradually drew out his Beretta 70 pistol and took shaky aim at the mighty and menacing airborne monster looming directly overhead.

Suddenly, he was wholly irradiated—and blinded—by a dazzling Spectrolab NightSun search light!

"Do not shoot, Mister Hazard!" a thunderously loud, mannish voice boomed above him from the helicopter's external avionics loudspeaker. "We're US Special Forces! This aircraft is CIA–operated!"

Sagging against the rocky shore, completely spent, Hazard winced hard behind his upraised hand, straining to lift up his bleary eyes to contemplate the demonic, infernally floating machine in utter disbelief—like some nightmarish hallucination.

"That's right, son!" another much more familiar and welcoming voice broke in to announce himself with his instantly recognizable Southern drawl. "This is your good Texan buddy, Felix Lighter! And I've come to take you home!"

Overcome by shock and dismay, Mark Hazard grinned a grisly smile and chuckled to himself, a deeply soul–sick chuckle; and for the first time since his boyhood, he broke down, and his blue–grey eyes welled out as grudging tears streaked his sunken cheeks.

SIX:
INTO
THE
SALT
PIT

High up overhead, the Mi–8 helicopter hovered over the embattled forces far off below though the fighting was already abating.

"Go back!" Mark Hazard demanded with a pained groan.

"Go back where?" asked his long–time CIA friend, Felix Lighter, his hawk–like face displaying a scrupulous expression.

"The dam—the southern end!"

"What the hell for?" he asked, aghast.

"To catch a rat who's run to ground—a militant!"

"What do we want with him?"

"He's key to this mess somehow."

"That's crazy!"

"This whole escapade's mad. EM said so!"

"That's gratitude for you!" Lighter griped. "I save your bacon for the umpteenth time—and all you can say to me is, go back to the damn...dam!"

"Thank you, Felix," Hazard condescended. "It's very, very good to see you again as well. Now get this rig back to the bloody dam before we lose him—and hand me a pair of fieldglasses!"

§

At Lighter's command, the Mi–8 helicopter's three–man crew—pilot, co–pilot, flight engineer—flew a steady circuit as the rotorcraft went the round of the dam's southern end. A pair of Special Forces soldiers, clad in their Operational Camouflage Pattern uniforms, manned the aircraft's two side–mounted, gas–operated, belt–fed PK machine guns chambered for the 7.62x54mmR rimmed cartridge. Its powerfully brilliant searchlight irradiated the ground below with a wandering beam of blinding brilliance.

"You're lucky our side's making short work of the opposition down there," Lighter told Hazard, "or else we might be dodging anti–aircraft fire!"

"I don't know what you're grousing about, Felix," Hazard said, focused on squinting intently through his binoculars. "This thing's armed with S–5 rockets."

"Show–off," Lighter wisecracked as Hazard grinned.

"Got you!" Hazard blurted out abruptly. "You bloody bastard!"

"You've spotted him?"

"Slipping into the power station!" Hazard nodded. "Put me down there!"

"Let us get him. You're in no condition to go chasing after this…militant."

"We need him *alive*—not blown to smithereens!"

"We'll capture him then," Lighter admonished him. "You're lucky you've lived to fight another day, my friend, so don't press your luck."

"The day isn't done yet, my friend," Hazard said, shaking his head. "Nor am I. Put me down there."

"It's your funeral," Lighter relented. "You're going to need a better gun than that water–logged Beretta of yours."

He produced a special, straight blowback–operated, double–action, semi–automatic pistol to hand over to Hazard: the Walther PPK!

"I know it's your second–favorite after that old equalizer of yours," he added with a warm smile.

"Most thoughtful, Felix," Hazard said, taking the gun and weighing it approvingly in his palm. Then he checked its eight–round magazine of .32ACP centerfire cartridges. "I'm speechless."

"It's all part of CIA's service–with–a–smile!" said Lighter mirthfully, gesturing to the helicopter's twelve stretchers seating twenty–two more stalwart soldiers. "There's a condition attached, of course. You take one of ours to go along with you."

"I'd like to volunteer, sir!" one strapping, young soldier

seated nearby spoke right up, bringing to bear his SIG Sauer MCX semi–automatic assault rifle. "To escort Mr. Hazard on this very important mission, sir!"

Mark Hazard and Felix Lighter both looked down their noses at each other, satirical smirks on their faces.

"Your chaperon!" Lighter suggested.

"That's what I like about you Yanks!" Hazard quipped finally. "You're always so...*gung–ho!*"

§

Tabqa Dam is a large, run–of–the–river hydroelectric generation plant possessing a comparatively small reservoir, or pondage. Its penstocks, or enclosed sluice–gate pipes, deliver river water to its hydro turbines. Shooting up some two hundred feet, the massive edifice encompassing the dam's power plant station towers roughly eight stories high. There was plenty of space atop the structure's flat roof for the M–8 helicopter to set down on.

Hazard and his US special forces guard readily found their way to a narrow rooftop doorway leading to a small service elevator, stepping directly inside. In its cramped compartment, a dual set of little two–button metal control boxes was attached to one of its walnut–paneled walls.

"The bottom one's for down, I hope," Hazard surmised, pressing the bottom button.

As if in reply, a little yellow light blinked on, the little elevator lurched to life and started its smooth and speedy descent—the bare cement surface passing by as they slid downward.

"We'll be sitting ducks as soon as this thing touches bottom," Hazard advised, "so take cover."

"Sir!"

"At all costs, try to take this villain alive—without endangering yourself, of course. He won't come quietly."

"Sir!"

As soon as it hit bottom, Hazard and his guard burst out of the little elevator in opposite directions, crouching low as they each took cover behind the nearest solid barrier.

Before them spread the expansive, high–ceilinged power plant station, sharply polished and shiny from being irradiated by brilliant lighting. A loud, big–sounding humming noise reverberated throughout the vast space. From one end to the other, set at evenly spaced intervals, stood its eight tall, Kaplan propeller–type water turbines with adjustable blades.

On either side, they slid together from one turbine to another in search of their elusive, militant quarry. Once they passed by a spacious, open chamber enclosing a gigantic, whirring generator and transformer, it wasn't long before a couple of rapidly fired pistol shots zinged toward them, ricocheting off the walls! Instinctively, Hazard bent his knee and promptly returned fire, setting his sights on the elevated metal gantry he sensed those shots came from! Then he retreated behind another of those great water turbines.

"What do you want here?" the militant shouted virulently.

"I told you at the castle," Hazard answered him, "to talk business."

"With that measly money of yours?"

"That was counterfeit, I'm afraid, so sorry about that."

"Deceiver!" the militant ranted. "Hundreds of thousands of innocent people will die if this dam collapses because of your interminable bombing!"

"We're not here to sabotage this dam," Hazard assured him, "I swear to you!"

"Deceiver! What do you want then?"

"To talk about those corsets."

"Imbecile! You came all this way—from wherever you came from—to talk about women's girdles!"

"We both know there's a lot more to it than that."

"And we'll both die before you ever find out anything about it!"

"We can pay you any amount of money you want for it."

"Do you really think that you can bribe one of the believers—one of the faithful?"

"It's not a bribe—it's a reward."

"For what?"

"For *being* faithful."

"You speak like a snake! Disbeliever!"

"Look," Hazard pleaded with the militant, "come out of hiding and let's talk. I don't want you hurt. The exits to this place have all been sealed off by now. And there's a trigger-happy Green Beret with a carbine here with me—and I don't want him to accidentally shoot you."

"Assassins!" the militant spouted wrathfully. "God is the greatest! God is the greatest!"

He fired rapidly and wildly in their direction—the bullets ricocheting indiscriminately—until his pistol clicked empty!

"That's a Makarov," Hazard told him knowingly, "and you've had your eight."

Guardedly, Hazard betrayed himself and sauntered over to the foot of the gantry's metal stairway, his gun at his hip.

"By the way," he added jauntily, introducing himself, "I never got your name. Mine's Hazard, Mark Hazard."

Unexpectedly, the militant leapt headlong from atop that gantry, pouncing upon Hazard from overhead—taking him unawares! Together, they tumbled to the slick floor, each struggling to lay their hands on Hazard's gun—the militant laying hold of it first!

It was a brief encounter. Hazard managed to deliver an elbow strike to the militant's head and slam his grip hand hard against the unyielding floor—the gun clattering across the slippery surface—before he went abruptly limp, sprawled unconscious.

Hazard lifted up his unsuspecting eyes to deliberately take the full measure of the tall and stout US special forces soldier hovering over them! Right after he'd just whacked the militant's head hard with his assault rifle's unfolded, 29–inch stock!

"Thank you!" Hazard said ironically, getting to his feet to stare down his nose at the militant's prone shape lying listless on the floor. "I just hope he's not brain–dead from a cracked skull."

"Sir!"

§

SALT PIT
DETENTION CENTER
CIA BLACK SITE
KABUL, AFGHANISTAN

That self–styled Salt Pit, also known as the dark prison, was a sprawling, isolated, 10–acre, clandestine CIA black site detention and interrogation center situated north of Kabul at the site of an old brick factory, surrounded by a desolate, mountainous landscape. Curtains and painted exterior windows kept it lightless—hence its dark designation. Clamorous music blared from loudspeakers throughout the three–story compound's cell block to keep prisoners sleep–deprived.

Inside one cold, stark cell, the captured militant, wearing an orange prison jump suit, sat shackled and strapped to a black–metal chair bolted to the floor.

Felix Lighter held up the stump of his right hand, gloved by a shiny steel hook, to the light—a bright square in the ceiling that glinted off the metal and turned even his straw–colored hair into golden wheat. That militant riveted his worried eyes on that steel hook as Lighter wiped it, regardfully, with a soft terry cloth.

"You brought me here to be interrogated by Captain Hook?" sniggered the militant.

"A scholar, he is!" remarked Lighter, just as facetious, glancing around at Mark Hazard, sitting nearby with a non–committal look on his face.

"I lost that after a shark bit it off!" recounted Lighter, pulling up his trouser cuff, exposing his prosthetic limb. "My left leg, too!"

"You disagreed with something that ate you!" snickered the militant.

"An intellectual, too!" remarked Lighter with a nod toward Hazard.

"Very funny," Lighter told the militant, "but I have a far more amusing saying when it comes to my steely little friend here: you'll disagree with something that *eviscerates* you! And by the time I'm through with you, you'll be singing soprano in nothing flat!"

"Mark," Lighter suggested, turning to Hazard, "maybe you should excuse us while we discuss ladies' girdles. I appreciate how much the sight of blood upsets you."

"Suits me," Hazard said agreeably, getting to his feet, "but before I go..."

Then he bowed down in front of the militant, letting a fist fly and slugging him hard in the gut, doubling him over with a loud groan of agony.

"I'd like to disembowel you myself for what you did to Yasin Salih!" Hazard growled irately, wrenching him violently by the neck with both hands. "But I take great comfort in knowing that you're going to rot in this hell–hole for a long time to come—and that you'll get plenty of rectal feeding tubes stuck up your arse to help you pass the time of day! Enjoy yourself!"

"Not to worry though," Lighter, bowing down alongside Hazard, remarked with mock assurance, "our esteemed president has ordered that we resort to only the nineteen interrogation methods outlined in the United States Army Field Manual."

"Of course," Lighter added forebodingly, standing erect and caressing his shiny steel hook with affected...affection, "those methods are open to considerable interpretation...and practice. We have no...red lines."

"I'll leave you to it then," said Hazard, turning on his heel to make his exit.

§

Hazard disapproved of the torture of prisoners, as a rule, but felt sorely tempted to making a strong exception in that murderous militant's case. Before long, though, Lighter met up with Hazard, rejoining him in the compound's checker–floored recreation room, furnished with a pair of rectangular, six–pocket Snooker tables covered with green baize cloth, where he waited expectantly.

"Well?"

"Relax!" Felix Lighter reassured his good friend with a beaming grin. "I've discovered the name and address of your mysterious corset–maker, as it were...and you're never, ever going to believe where it's located!"

SEVEN:
TEN BEAUTIFUL BRIDES

JOSEPH COVINO JR

Târgu Mureș
Transylvania International Airport
Romania

Shades of Count Dracula, vampires, or *Strigoi*—troubled spirits and undead creatures from folklore, said to have risen from their graves to survive by feeding on the vital essence of the living, attributed by Romanian mythology with the abilities to transform themselves into animals and become invisible to attain vitality from the blood of their victims!

Seeing Hazard off at the airport, Felix Lighter just couldn't resist cracking his sappy jokes about his being forewarned, and well–advised, to properly prepare for his trip by packing the most practical and life–saving supply of equipment: like garlic, crucifixes, and sharpened wooden stakes! Wiseass bastard! Such were some of the preposterous thoughts coming into Hazard's head as his sleek, narrow–body, twin engine jet engine Tarom Romanian Airlines Boeing 737–800 touched down at Târgu Mureș, Transylvania International Airport in central Romania.

After Syria, admittedly, it felt rather refreshing to return to the luxurious fleshpots of so–called civilization. Even the modernized structure of the airport's recently refurbished main terminal building proved soothing to Hazard's tired eyes—being saturated with neon blue, a shade of his favorite color. All of the picture windows of its lattice–like front facade were framed in blue. Inside, even the polished, shiny, whitewashed arrival–and–departure areas were duly furnished with round–topped glass tables and blue lounge chairs. Brightly emblazoned in yellow across its blue rooftop canopy were the words: *Transylvania Airport!*

He'd deplaned and was prepared to keep his appointment with the proprietors of *Castle Corsetry*, Transylvania's premier...corsetmakers! It was still hard for Hazard to be-

83

lieve, as a secret agent for Her Majesty's Secret Service, that he was actually hot on the trail of what he'd ironically christened to be…killer corsets!

It was back to Dracula country again, though, once Hazard's dark–uniformed chauffeur—a tall, gaunt, and glowering man who reminded him, rather scurrilously, of actor Max Schreck's *Nosferatu!*—showed up to drive him the roughly forty–two miles to Turda, a city in Cluj County, Transylvania, in southeastern Romania. Cluj International Airport was just about twenty–four miles from Turda, true, but Hazard had preferred to alight at Transylvania International. It was a smooth, comfortable, and uneventful one–and–a–half hour ride to their destination in the futuristic, Dacia Bigster—a gleaming silver, five–door SUV with front–four–wheel drive, and powered on a Renault CMF–B platform with a permanent–magnet synchronous motor: an electric car!

§

VILLA MANDEL

Villa Mandel was a graceful, two–story, early twentieth–century structure built, architecturally, in the Viennese Secession style. Hazard, who could speak both French and German, recalled that Mandel meant almond in German.

Hazard's chauffeur steered the Dacia Bigster through the double wrought iron gates that breached the tall, gray, granitic wall surrounding the villa's elegant, burnt almond edifice. They went the round of its gravel driveway until pulling up to its grandiose entrance. Hazard fell out into the warm and dry summer air of the city's continental climate.

Hazard's chauffeur carried his lightweight Hartmann Skymate suitcase up the short flight of seven marble steps that rose to the double–glass doors framed in gleaming gold. Hazard draped his light–weight camel–hair overcoat

84

with over–buttressed shoulders over one arm. Mounting the steps, they stepped together inside the bright and cheery vestibule overhung with the ornate and gilded chandelier. Their feet scuffed across an expansively polished and shiny floor as they stepped up to the foot of a grand and winding staircase, carpeted in maroon and sidled by a wrought iron railing with ornate, black fretwork.

It was there that Hazard was greeted abruptly by two pairs of beautiful and bountiful feminine bosoms—or, rather, by the two beautiful and bountiful young women baring their ample, fleshy, and partly exposed breasts to him!

One, whose curly, coal–black tresses cascaded past her shoulders, was clad in gaudy red. One, whose curly, fiery scarlet tresses cascaded past her shoulders, was clad in garish black. Both women were possessed of pallid and pinkish complexions, high foreheads, large eyes set beneath straight, thin brows, chiseled cheekbones, large noses, thin rouged lips, and small chins. Both buxom, full–fleshed women were wrapped up in laced, form–fitting white bodices.

Sauntering leisurely down that staircase—their hands lovingly clasped and held upright between them in a conspicuous display of affection and attachment—the voluptuous pair alighted together at the foot of those carpeted steps.

"Welcome to Villa Mandel, Mr. Hazard," the dark–haired one hailed him solemnly, introducing themselves. "I'm Marie Heller and this is my life partner, Liona Heller. We are the proprietresses of this establishment."

An erotic beauty mark spotted the right corner of her sensual mouth, he noticed right off. Completely captivated, Hazard looked agape at this exceptional pair of resplendent young women.

"Are you well, Mr. Hazard?" Marie Heller asked him gently.

"I'm sorry," Hazard apologized with a slight bow, trying to act courtly. "Forgive me for staring, my dear lovely ladies, but for a moment I actually thought that I had arrived at the pearly gates!"

"You were perhaps expecting to see Saint Peter?" Marie Heller remarked with a slight scowl.

"Or your fairy godmother?" Liona Heller chimed in coquettishly.

"Quite frankly," Hazard answered, holding up his hands resignedly, "I didn't know what to expect. But you do look like you could hold the keys to the kingdom!"

Hesitantly, he held out his hand, offering to press his against theirs.

"I'm very pleased to make your acquaintance," he bid them.

In response, they both recoiled, moving back from him, embracing each other tightly about the waist. Hazard promptly dropped his hand down by his side, abashed.

"The only key that we hold is the one to your guest suite, Mr. Hazard," Marie Heller volunteered, her brow furrowed by her frown as she reached out to him.

"Of course," Hazard relented, holding out his hand once more, palm upwards, to accept the clinking silver key hitched to a tiny chain attached to the round, gold medal engraved in black with the number eight!

"You may frequent any of the villa's strictly communal areas at all times, Mr. Hazard," Marie Heller informed him rather sternly. "Your meals shall be served in your suite until your private showing scheduled for tomorrow afternoon, following lunch. *Max* will show you to your suite. Enjoy your visit with us, Mr. Hazard."

Agape, Hazard did a sudden double–take of his laconic chauffeur, still standing over him like a silent sentinel. He *was* Max, after all! If these two curvaceous vixens suddenly sprouted sharp fangs in the dead of night, Hazard thought ironically, then perhaps he ought to load his Beretta with silver bullets made from molten crucifixes!

"Thank you both for your kindness and hospitality," he told them with a slight, courtly bow.

In response, they merely nodded—in intensely taciturn silence!

§

It was more of a stage than a fashion catwalk or runway, but it was the ornamental platform situated in the simple and unpretentious parlor where Villa Mandel's girls were scheduled to model specially for Hazard their latest line of tailor–made...corsets! It was a low–set, raised platform, made of polished wooden paneling, in the shape of a bowed but level disk. At its rear, on either side, rose a twin pair of Gothic columns—from which protruded brightly flaring, gilt lamps—that buttressed the decorative canopy overhead. Its backdrop was a curved, Gothic–decorated partition that glowed dimly with a lattice–work of eerily–colored lighting. A narrow crimson carpet led downstage to a separate but smaller, stepped platform in the shape of three stacked concentric circles. Hazard sat directly downstage in a plush, padded chair placed at its frontward base. Seated at either of his elbows were the Heller girls.

"How did you find your accommodation, Mr. Hazard?" Marie Heller ventured to ask.

"Most...accommodating," he answered, absentminded, watching the stage expectantly. "Yes, very agreeable, thank you!"

She nodded with a slight smile in acknowledgment. She held up a vibrant, iridescent peacock's train feather to her left eye, regarding him mindfully through its coloured eyespot!

Hazard thought back upon his room's various amenities—in particular the minibar, of the absorption refrigerator variety, stocked full of several bottles of *Slivovitz* plum brandy from the Banat region straddling Eastern and Central Europe—as well as the available, flavorful meals consisting

87

of traditional staples such as sour ciorbă soup, chiftele meat balls, grilled minced mititei meat rolls, sarmale minced meat, şniţel or schnitzel, and tochitură, pan–fried cubed pork; and those were just the meats! There was also an assortment of stuffed cabbage rolls, pilaf, and of course ghiveci, a vegetable stew and Romania's national dish. Various cheeses and salads native to the county were offered besides.

Served for this special occasion—and event—was simply vin, the country's preferred drink, a traditional Romanian red wine from the Romanian–Moldavian grape, fetească neagră. Hazard's partially filled glass swirled with the deeply red–coloured libation that sparkled with ruby shades. Sipping sparingly, he savored the sweetness of the wine's rich and smooth black currant flavour.

"By way of introduction, Mr. Hazard," Marie Heller addressed him directly to attract his attention, "I should explain that we offer only high–quality, handmade and unique designs built to last. In a world focused on quantity, and keen on the disposable, we create every piece of clothing with care and attention to detail. That gives each garment a sense of value quite uncommon in the modern fashion industry. We call it *slow* fashion."

"I should expect no less," Hazard approved. "Every garment is made to order then?"

"Made–to–measure, we prefer to say."

"But of course, dear."

"We never use standard sizes," she clarified, pursing her lips with a slightly perturbed expression. "Each woman's body is unique, so any attempt to make them fit in narrow boxes leaves a lot of bodies out of the equation."

"Dear," she added with an emphatic smirk.

"I do admire your ideals," Hazard said, wincing at her slight rebuff.

"We cater to clients of all shapes and forms," she went on pridefully, "by carefully crafting garments built to fit each client like a glove. We create a new pattern for each individual client, made to fit her unique measurements, thus accentuating and complementing the shapes and beauty of each body. We don't believe in...*curated* figures."

"Nor do I," Hazard agreed.

"Good," she said with favor. "Shall we now contemplate these ideals in their more corporeal and appreciable forms?"

"By all means," Hazard said, enthusiastic, "let's please do!"

Marie Heller signaled a shadowed figure waiting in the wings of the small stage with a slight gesture of her peacock feather. Then the parlor's house lights dimmed, fading to partial darkness, as a hushed but anxious stillness settled over the room.

§

It was a passing fashion show of sorts, fleeting but flamboyant, but more spectacular and impressive than Hazard could have ever anticipated. Paraded ceremoniously before him, with dramatic flair and flourish, were ten of the most beautiful and breathtaking young cosmopolitan women he had ever seen—all voluptuous, all alluring, all wantonly flaunting their well–favored faces and full–fleshed figures. And all wore nothing except scantily–clad corsets of various colors and configurations! Transylvanian folk music, executed by cimbalom, double bass, kontra, and violin, blared over loudspeakers.

Back and forth, up and down that brightly lit stage, those ten gorgeous girls sauntered leisurely, each in their turn—skillfully strutting their steps, suggestively swinging their hips in fluid and languid motion. And as their rather erotic procession carried on, their names and countries of origin were dramatically announced: Amira of Austria; Minera of Belgium; Nesrine of Canada; Farzana of Finland; Zahera of France; Hafsa of Germany; Haleema of Malaysia; Zara of

Morocco; Zohura of Norway; Samra of Singapore.

Surreptitiously—with casual flicks of his wrist—Hazard took pictures of each and every last stunning and devastatingly beautiful young girl with the miniature digital camera hidden in his silver Rolex Sea Dweller wrist–watch! Christ! he thought—these comely girls were all doubtless Brides of the Islamic State!

"Absolutely sublime!" Hazard, utterly mesmerized, muttered in admiration.

"Of course," Marie Heller reminded him as a belated, forgotten afterthought. "each unique and extraordinary design is necessarily accompanied by a unique and extraordinary young woman!"

"I see," Hazard said distractedly, smitten most by the young Moroccan girl named Zara.

And, curiously enough, Zara noticed his conspicuous preoccupation with her; and her own conspicuous expression seemed to wordlessly betray that she was equally taken with him!

EIGHT:
LOVING THE SACRIFICIAL LAMB

"Pick up the torch of liberation and struggle, for with each heartbeat our nation is taking form. Your body is the fuel that sustains the fire."—Rebel Poem

M ark Hazard, completely rapt, gawped at the empty spot on the stage that the comely Moroccan model named Zara had just vacated. Already, her eye–filling image was preoccupying his mind: her long, wavy, sable black hair flowing thickly down her bare back to frizzy extremes; her golden brown oval face and features—the almond–shaped eyes set deep beneath the dark, broadly arched brows; the slightly long but straight nose; the high, perfectly sculptured cheekbones; and the full and wide mouth with the lush lips that parted often to tempt ceaseless kisses; and the well formed, bronzed body of silken flesh and lithesome limbs.

"Did you see a design that struck your fancy?" Marie Heller asked him, intruding upon his deep reflection.

"Yes...well," he stammered, coming back to his senses, "they're all perfectly splendid...but..."

"But?"

"Given the appreciable amount of money that we've discussed," he clarified, turning businesslike, "my principals at Transworld Corporation are interested in the most magnetic design—the one capable of strongly attracting not only spectators but tangible things as well."

"Indeed? What sorts of things?"

"Airborne objects, per example," Hazard answered after momentary deliberation.

"I see."

"Apropo that," Hazard continued, "my principals would prefer that we personally inspect an operational prototype of the design before we could commit to any substantial investment in that commodity."

"Yes," she assented, nodding assuredly, "that could be arranged. Of course, strict security protocol would have to be observed."

"Of course," Hazard readily agreed. "As a duly authorized representative of Transworld Corporation, I'm at your

93

complete disposal."

"Good," she approved. "Have you ever experienced *halotherapy?*"

"Halotherapy?" Hazard repeated, surprised. "No, I can't say that I have. What is it?"

"It's a form of alternative medicine that utilizes salt treatment," she explained, "perfectly harmless but potentially very beneficial."

"Salt treatment? For what?"

"Respiratory ailments, mostly."

"I haven't any, I'm afraid."

"Oh yes, you do," she said contrarily with a suggestive smile, "if you care to inspect the desired merchandise, that is."

"Then yes," Hazard corrected himself, playing along cooperatively, "I do. I most definitely do!"

"Good," she approved again. "I shall issue you a complimentary pass. Max will drive you to your appointment tomorrow."

I can't wait, Hazard thought, smirking satirically to himself.

"Thank you," he told her instead, smiling warmly.

§

At just about midnight, Hazard heard a light rapping, tapping at his chamber door—most reminiscent of Edgar Allan Poe's stylistic and supernatural narrative poem, the *Raven* from January 1845!

"Who is it?" he asked, going up to the door but stepping to one side of it, wrapping up his gripped Beretta pistol in a bath towel.

"Zara," came the whispered reply.

"Good evening," said Hazard, his brows raised quizzically as he budged open the door, peering through the crack

94

at her stunning visage. Beneath a long, black, visna cape, she wore absolutely nothing but a long, flowing, gossamer nightgown. "Isn't this the witching hour?"

"I must see you!" she said with some urgency.

"Must you? Wasn't there something about keeping to the common areas of the villa?"

"Unless you're invited in by someone."

"I see," he said playfully. "Forgive my appalling manners then. By all means, yes, do come in!"

As he stepped aside, she swept past him, turning on her heel to confront him once inside; he shut the door behind her.

"I was just about to take a bath," he said, explaining away the folded towel—with the hidden handgun—which he plunked down on the nearest tabletop. "What can I do for you—dare I ask?"

"You can tell me what you seemed to find so captivating about me at the corset show today," she said seriously.

"Is that all?" Hazard quibbled, making light of the question. "I found all of you lovely ladies quite charming—and captivating."

"You know what I mean."

"Yes," he relented, "I know what you mean. All you need do for an answer to that, really, is look into any looking glass."

"You're so frightfully obvious, Mr. Hazard," she said, a sardonic scowl furrowing her brow. "Anyone can be attracted by a perception of beauty."

"Perhaps," said Hazard with a shrug. "It's a rare and subtle thing, though, to be inspired by someone to experience the *feeling* of beauty. That's something else again."

"Yes, it is," she said, coming up close to him, gazing directly into his eyes, her voice tempered by the timbre of surrender. "I'll help you draw that bath now."

"I'll let you…if you'll call me Mark."

Slowly, Hazard folded her in his arms. Her arms reached

round his neck. He slid one hand down her back to the curve of her spine, pressing her tight against him, one of his thighs wedging her legs apart. Her eyes were glistening hot. Their mouths smashed and they kissed deeply, passionately. He clutched her hair with his other hand so that he could hold her mouth exactly where he wanted it. They kissed again, long and lustfully. His free hand roamed and clung to one of her warm and swelling breasts, its firm nipple peaked between his softly exploring fingers. Slowly, he undid the thin thread loosely fastening the top of her flimsy gown. She looked down at her heaving breasts, soft and supple, rising and falling as their fine and fleshy curves were gradually bared. Then, softly caressing her face with both hands, he slid his warm palms down the length of her silken neck, across her strong shoulders, and down further still, plunging into the deep cleft of her fervidly swollen bosom—until, finally, her sheer gown fell away and tumbled lightly to the floor!

§

Hung low on the ocher–colored wall, above the beige headboard of the broad bed where they had made both tender and delectable love—where no wrong or harm had been done between them—was a large and rather erotic impressionistic painting depicting a feminine nude. She was portrayed seated on her haunches with her back facing the viewer, her head tilted jauntily to one side so that her long, dark and wavy hair hung down along the elongated cleft of her bare back, reaching to her plump and rounded bare bottom.

For all Mark Hazard knew, that comely and curvaceous young woman so carnally portrayed, could have stepped right out of that explicit painting and then into the brightly turquoise hot tub in which he presently sat, warmly immersed—and could have become the remarkably comely, curvaceous, and naked young woman named Zara, who was sponging his bare, muscular chest with soapy, warm water.

If Zara was colluding to elevate suicide bombing to a far more elaborate and sophisticated art form, Hazard thought to himself ironically, the A.L.E.R.T. system of detection—which stands for *A*lone and Nervous, *L*oose and Bulky Clothing, *E*xposed Wires, *R*igid Midsection, and *T*ightened Hands—could scarcely be expected to ever expose her!

"Are you really aware of what we are," Zara asked him gravely, "my dear Mark?"

"Sacrificial lambs sent out on suicide missions," Hazard answered, pulling a long face. "Sadly."

"No!" Zara protested, raising her voice. "We're warrior women! Not victims! So don't dare to pity us!"

"It's just inconceivable to me that you could sacrifice yourself—killing yourself to kill others," he commiserated.

"Because you can conceive of only killing for a cause—not dying for it!"

"Is your cause really worth such sacrifice?"

"Our shared causes are all very much the same—our struggles for freedom, freedom from foreign oppression—and the liberation of our homelands from outside occupation forces."

"Can such sacrifice accomplish those causes with such violence?"

"*Jihad* is a holy and just war, my dear Mark," Zara said with devout fervor. "Our enemies are appreciably more powerful than we are—our cause seemingly impossible. We are then driven to desperation. We die to destroy. But we die with dignity. It's the only means left to us."

"How did you become so radicalised?"

"We're not radicalised—we're wronged and we're outraged! You must have an aversion to injustice to ever understand the compulsion to avenge it."

"It seems to me that you've been misled to believe that your life isn't worth living—that it's valued less than others."

"Self–sacrifice is the ultimate act of commitment—commitment to a cause and utter faith in it. That's more than worthy."

"Tragically," Hazard retorted, "it's your last act as well."

"It will bring about the last of our oppressors!"

"Have you no regard for the innocent casualties you kill in the process?" he asked her pointedly.

"As much regard as you foreign interlopers have for installing your repressive, puppet regimes for the purpose of exploiting our oil! As much regard as you have for indiscriminately bombing into oblivion our freedom–fighters who resist your forced occupation of our homelands!"

"I have nothing to do with any of that, my dear."

"Have you ever been in love, Mark?"

"Of course—deeply and irrevocably. Why?"

"Because you're incapable of accepting that killing yourself and others for a cause is an act of someone who *loves* life!"

"But I thought that loving Muslim women were supposed to stay at home, give birth to children, and care for their families—not blow themselves up for political causes."

"Self–sacrifice is the most all–giving, all–consuming love you can express. Until the time comes that you are ready to give up your life for the sake of a cause that's greater than yourself, you will never know such a love."

"At the risk of disillusioning you," Hazard said appeasingly, "the sole interest my corporation has in any of this business is a hefty return on its investment—profit."

"Then you're neither spy nor sympathizer?" Zara asked with a mocking smile.

"Is that what you were sent to find out?"

"I'm not a woman to be sent," Zara admonished him ominously. "Just be careful at your halotherapy visit tomorrow. Other suspected spies have gone for the cure but have never come back."

"I'm much obliged," Hazard said thankfully. "I'll be on my guard then."

"If you're not a woman to be sent," he asked, turning mischievous, "then what kind of woman are you?"

Zara sank back against the facing side of the tub, heaving a heavy but satisfied sigh. Crossing her arms, she embraced herself, her curvaceous bosom cleaved tightly together, partly exposed in the sudsy water.

"I'm the kind of woman," she hissed through her teeth, lifting up her languid eyes and gazing over at Hazard, a lascivious look in those eyes, "expecting to be pleased—again."

NINE:
FLYING
THE
COCOON

Max, Hazard's peculiar chauffeur, pulled up the Dacia Bigster to a remarkably curious structure of concrete, metal, and glass—a great, gray shell building constructed of a twin pair of capsized, arched, concentric half–cylinders—the outer envelope being made of fluted concrete, the inner envelope made of corrugated glass. Max idled the SUV to drop off Hazard in front of the unique structure with a pledge to return to pick him up later on. Hazard paused, lifting up his eyes to contemplate with wonder the structure's uncommon exterior contours. Finally, he pressed forward to pass through the revolving glass–door that comprised the structure's front entrance.

Inside, Hazard set foot on a smooth, polished gray floor, crossing over to a creamy white–coloured reception(*"receptie"*) desk. High up, overhead, hovered the pavilion's vaulted dome. Circular apertures in the lofty dome shed bright light from above.

"Hello," he addressed the ethereal beauty of a young girl posted there, "I'm Mark Hazard. I've come for my appointment."

"Hello, Mr. Hazard," she greeted him graciously with a genteel gesture of her delicate hand. "I'm Gabriela. You're expected. Follow me, please."

She was tall, slender, and pale, her long tresses reaching in auburn braids to the middle of her back. Her wide eyelids and thin lips were darkly rouged. She wore a chic, black Elisabeth dress with a white linen chemise, and sateen ribbon bows at the shoulders. Its slightly plunging neckline was fringed with delicate black lace, partly exposing the tantalizing curves of her small and supple bosom. She led the way, sauntering languidly, through the arched entry to a cobalt blue portal.

Through that portal, the girl led Hazard to a short flight of four steps that mounted the foot of a narrow, wood–paneled, short–spanned foot–bridge—slightly bowed in the middle and bordered on either side by low–set metal railings—that cut a passage through a cragged cavern. At evenly spaced intervals, the bridge was partitioned by lofty, wooden, inverted V–shaped arches.

"What in the world is this?" Hazard asked, aghast.

"It's a salt cave, Mr. Hazard," his fetching hostess told him.

"A salt cave?" Hazard exclaimed, idling in the middle of the bridge to lean on its metal railing.

"Transylvanian salt deposits formed more than thirteen million years ago," she recounted, "and they've been mined for hundreds of years since."

"That's certainly something to think about the next time you're sprinkling your *pâté*," Hazard quipped.

"Because of its unique microclimate," she continued with a polite smile, "salt inhalation can be beneficial therapy for people afflicted with respiratory conditions."

"Micro–climate?"

"Salt–infused air inside of a humid cave having curative qualities that can treat respiratory ailments like asthma, bronchitis, or sinusitis. Breathing salt vapor has been practiced since the twelfth century."

"I must admit," Hazard conceded, "I've heard of salt bringing good luck, but never better health."

"Halotherapy is derived from speleotherapy," Gabriela elucidated in more depth, "the treatment in the natural salt caves, mined for rock salt. These salt deposits were formed as horizontal salt beds in ancient oceans and were later buried deeply beneath sediments as mountains eroded. This therapy has been practiced in salt caves of Eastern and Central Europe for over 150 years. During the late 18th century the doctors noticed that the workers of salt mining industry never suffered from bronchial or lung diseases, which they realized was due to high salt aerosol content in the mines."

"Never?"

"Rarely," she corrected herself. "Men working in the salt mines rarely suffered from respiratory problems. The air pressure and circulation in the salt mine, saturated with dry salt particles which were disbursed in the air through chiseling, grinding and hammering the salt, was believed to have caused the healing effects on people with pulmonary and respiratory problems."

"This therapy, I take it, has been adapted for modern applications."

"In a modern version of this ancient therapy, *halogenerators* are being used in a controlled environment to offer the benefits of the natural deposits found in rock salt. These minerals, when concentrated in an enclosed area with stable air temperature, humidity, and the absence of airborne pollutants, offer tremendous relief to the respiratory system. These salt particles are then minute enough to penetrate deep into the lung tissue."

"Fascinating. How does this therapy actually work?"

"The procedure is very simple," she explained, "you enter the salt room and make yourself comfortable. While you relax and breathe naturally the micro–climate clears and cleanses the respiratory system. Positive ions are converted to negative ions which strengthens the immune system. There are no allergens or microbes so the immune system gets a chance to rest. After this, the defenses begin to work alone. Many of our problems start when the immune system breaks down and, because we are exposed to so much pollution, it is ever more important to clean the lungs in order to avoid developing asthma or terminal illnesses. Salt therapy acts as an anti–oxidant reducing inflammation in the airways."

With another taciturn gesture of her delicate, pale hand, Gabriela invited Hazard to follow her to the other end of the bowed foot–bridge.

There, another portal opened up to a spacious salt room,

whose curved ceiling and cavernous walls, carved out of hefty salt–blocks, were wholly aglow with brightly luminous orange hues. Placed all around its salt–flaked floor, arranged neatly in orderly rows, were the room's sole furnishings: numerous lounge chairs—cushioned and padded for reclining at length. Together, the two stepped inside the expansive, hollow salt cave–chamber. Pebble–sized salt crystals, scattered all around, crunched underfoot.

"Consider this to be your salt sanatorium, Mr. Hazard," the girl suggested.

"Going mad for salt seems a little extreme," Hazard quipped. "I think that I'd rather consider it to be my salt *spa*."

"Perfectly acceptable," Gabriela approved, and with another taciturn gesture of her hand, she showed the way to a cragged recess of the salt cave as she expounded further about salt treatment.

"It's a dry therapy," she went on. "The halogenerator disperses, very precisely, pure ground up sodium chloride aerosol into the air, which mimics the environment of the natural salt cave and allows you to breathe its benefits."

Just then, they stepped up to a remarkably curious, futuristic–looking object, situated in a corner of the salt cave, that looked like an over–sized, Plexiglas bivalve clam shell! Its lower, bottom half was a solid pearly white. Its upper, top half was a transparent canopy that hung open like a yawning, hinged lid. Inside, the contraption was lined with a cushioned, turquoise seat.

"Good lord!" exclaimed Hazard. "What is this?"

"A Salt Cocoon," Gabriela related, "a small, compact salt chamber which is designed for individual salt therapy."

"This," she added forebodingly, "is your end destination."

"Is it?" he said, incredulous. "Well, I'm damned! It looks quite claustrophobic. Am I expected to sit inside that thing?"

"It's perfectly harmless, Mr. Hazard," she assured him. "It's equipped with a dry salt aerosol generator—essentially a portable and adjustable halogenerator. This one has a pre–set regimen of operation with a mild level of salt–aerosol concentration."

"It's safe?"

"Pefectly. The lid does not lock. You can exit the cocoon at any time should you feel the slightest discomfort."

"I suppose I'll just have to take your word for that."

"If you expect to inspect the apparatus that you've come to see," she told him with a grimly resolute tone of voice, "yes."

"Carry on," Hazard agreed with a sedate shrug of his shoulders as he climbed, unshakably, into the cocoon, settling into its comfortable, upright seat.

"Simply relax," Gabriela exhorted him as she slowly closed down the base–hinged, translucent canopy, "breathe easily and gently inhale the micron–sized salt particles."

From his new vantage point inside that seemingly airtight compartment, those outer walls encompassing him emanated their faint, apricot–coloured glow. Hazard's hand went instinctively to the Beretta pistol holstered tight beneath his armpit, reaching reassuringly for its grip in case he was forced to shoot his way out of that limpid canopy. He wondered whether that hologenerator would knock him out, rendering him unconscious, with some sort of anesthetic or narcotic vapor—some sleeping gas. To the contrary, he felt quite awake and alert—not drowsy or sleepy at all—and breathed effortlessly, his airways and lungs feeling remarkably clear. As the seconds turned into minutes and a little time elapsed, the compartment's humid and moist interior fumed, and its see–through canopy started to cloud over with the gaseous, salt–aerosol vapor. Then Hazard suddenly realized that he forgot altogether to ask Gabriela just how long he was supposed to sit inside the damn thing!

Hazard was just about to push open the cocoon's canopy when the entire contraption lurched abruptly backwards—as if sliding smoothly on tracks! A partition in the salt–block wall behind it suddenly slid aside! With the clangorous hiss of hydraulic machinery, the whole cocoon was shifted full–tilt through the gaping hole in the wall! No sooner had the cocoon passed through the breach did that solid partition slide shut after it! It promptly ground to an abrupt halt! Its misty canopy flew wide open!

Hovering over Hazard, all of a sudden, was the most massive and muscular man he'd ever seen or encountered. A mighty Romanian weight–lifter if ever there was one! Powerfully–built and incredibly strong, the huge, hulking, human behemoth deliberately bowed down and—clinching him tightly by his lapels—hoisted Hazard bodily into mid-air, feet and legs dangling, like a helplessly broken doll!

TEN:
FIGHT
TO
THE
DEATH

Mark Hazard lifted up his eyes, thunderstruck, taking the measure of the mammoth Romanian strong man; who was, indeed, clad in a muscle shirt and sweatpants. He was the most threatening and intimidating muscleman Hazard had ever come in contact with—quite literally as the mighty he–man gently stiff–armed Hazard against a wet, granitic wall; after he'd put him down, of course. Without a word, the he–man reached promptly into Hazard's coat to expertly extract his Beretta pistol, tucking it tight into his own waistband.

"Help yourself," Hazard said sedately, not daring to resist.

Then, with a taciturn gesture of his outstretched hand, the mighty titan pointed a listless finger in the downward direction where he intended Hazard to descend to. Downward?

Looking around, Hazard finally discerned that they were both standing atop the metal landing to a protracted, railed, steel stairway that plummeted deep into the subterranean bowels of the earth. Before them, that protracted stairway sloped gradually downward, cutting a roughhewn passage through a cramped and tilted tunnel that was brightly lit, at evenly spaced intervals, by arched belts of luminescent lamps installed in the tunnel's curved ceiling.

Once more, the muscleman pointed—that time more emphatically. Preceding the strong man, Hazard started off with a shrug of his shoulders, leading the way downward. Their deliberate but slow climb down that steep stairway took them nearly 148 feet at a nearly 50–foot gradient for a protracted total of 107 steps—divided by other metal landings along the way!

At the foot of that protracted, confined stairway they arrived at another, horizontal but cramped tunnel that cut its gradually curved passage through the roughhewn gallery— likewise brightly lit at intervals, its wet walls glistening

111

from being saturated with clammy humidity. Together, they trudged another 377 feet through the muggy passageway, its gritty footpath incrusted with a granular overlay.

Finally, they emerged at a lofty wooden balcony—suspended in midair from the cavernous walls—stretching to a telescopic point a long way off in the shadowed distance. Beneath the sheer balcony, bordering the perimeter like a wooden gangway, the limestones plummeted through a yawning chasm yet another 262 feet! Along the cavernous walls and marbled ceiling hung cascading, neon chandeliers and jutting stalactites of salt, trickling with a blue–tinged glow.

Far off below them, the vast, vaulted, underground gallery opened up with a gaping, parallelepiped shape and a 160–foot trapezoidal canopy. At the end of the balcony, the mighty muscleman pointed the way to a final flight of zigzagging, wooden stairs that descended the 278 feet through the yawning breach in the gallery that was 164 feet wide!

At the foot of those stairs, a remarkably eccentric looking character, sporting a simple rumpled shirt and vest, stepped up to Hazard. He had a pudgy oval face, his broad forehead crowned by a messy mop of dark hair. His dark, bead–like eyes were set deep beneath long but thin, arched brows. His beaky nose hooked over his small mouth's thin upper lip.

"My name's Stanislaw Boczkowski," he introduced himself mirthfully, holding out his hand to press Hazard's. "I'm here to show you what you've come so far to see."

"I'm much obliged," Hazard said thankfully. "Forgive me, though, but what is this place?"

"This is a salt mine, Mr. Hazard, inactive," the Polish pipsqueak explained with a throwaway gesture of both his hands. "You're standing some four hundred feet underground, Mr. Hazard. The temperature is kept at a steady fifty–three degrees Fahrenheit year–round with about eighty percent humidity. These conditions are perfect for sun haters—like the traditional residents of Transylvania—but also optimum for halotherapy, the complementary health treatment in which people with respiratory problems spend time in humid, salt–infused air."

"So I gathered from Gabriela, the girl upstairs."

"Yes, she's most efficient."

"This way," the squat man who called himself Boczkowski gestured again, leading on nearby to a broad metal pedestal, brightly illuminated, supporting an artist's lay figure—a fiberglass female mannequin torso draped, in turn, with that portentous corset! Except that the spiral boning and busks of this particular support garment were alive and brightly pulsating with a glowing kaleidoscope of variegated, multi–colored fiber optics!

"It's all about missile guidance, Mr. Hazard," the Pole started to expound with his most erudite tone of voice, "controlling it and manipulating it from afar—which can prove to be very problematic given the vast variety of methods, or systems, of guiding a missile to its intended target."

"I can imagine," commented Hazard.

"Of course," he clarified, "guidance systems get divided into different categories according to whether they're designed to attack moving or fixed—that is, stationary targets."

"The trajectory that a missile takes while attacking a moving target being more dependent upon the target's movement," Hazard surmised.

"Quite so," the Pole nodded. "Then there are certain subsystems that determine the missile's category of guidance system. For our purposes, *homing guidance*—also known as proportional navigation—is the most relevant category since the guidance computers are in the missile itself. PN or Pro-Nav, as we call it, is a guidance principle used in some form or another by most homing air target missiles."

"Interesting."

"Then comes the type of navigational guidance system

itself—whether pre–set, inertial, resorting to accelerometers or gyroscopes, celestial, terrestrial, or even GPS."

"You're beginning to blind me with science, professor," Hazard said dryly with a slight nod toward the corset torso. "What about this thing then?"

"This ingenious device harks back to the simplest of radar homing devices," the Pole explained with conspicuous pride, "since even cruise missiles like the Tomahawk are equipped with a radar altimeter. So this device acts like a *remote* active radar homing missile guidance system!"

"Incredible!"

"Indeed," he elucidated further. "It improves upon and refines that electronic countermeasure concept known as radar deception—using a transponder to send out radio frequency signals to interfere with the operation of radar by saturating its receiver with false information."

"As in false targets—or decoys—for the sacrificial purpose of re–directing guided missiles toward those targets! My God!"

"It's an innovation of active phased array radar utilizing solid–state microelectronics—and an amplifier–transmitter capable of performing the functions of both receiver and transmitter."

Mark Hazard stood in awe of the corset torso, staring at it open–mouthed, his face reflecting its flickering, rainbow–hued incandescence.

"Unbelievable," he muttered.

"Suffice it to say that it works!" the Pole proclaimed with a definite finality. "Precisely how it works shall of necessity remain our trade secret!"

"And you're the inventor of this device?"

"Me?" the Pole chuckled aloud, bursting with abrupt laughter as he pinched his little ear lobe. "Oh my! Dear me, no! I'm merely the humble tailor who outfits these corsets with these devices! The inventor you want is Gustaf Klein, he's in Stockholm. But I'm afraid you won't be meeting him."

"Oh, what makes you say that?"

"Because," the Pole answered ironically, "my dear Mr. Hazard—of the British Secret Service—you'll be dead!"

Without warning, the monstrous Romanian muscle-man, who'd been hovering over Hazard from behind, drawing nearer, furtively, the more engrossed he became with the resplendent, prismatic apparatus on display, hammered the nape of Hazard's neck with a crashing wallop of his huge fist—laying him out cold!

§

Mark Hazard blinked his eyes open, squinting hard as he gradually returned to conscious awareness. Strangely, he felt the sensation of being levitated in midair, his legs and feet dangling at a hurtful angle. He sensed he was still in motion somehow or other. Bright streaks of light flashed across his face at deliberate and steadily spaced intervals. He stirred slightly, shaking his head awake to clear his senses.

Good God! He'd been hoisted onto the broad hip of the muscleman, who had a firm hold of his waistband to balance him there. They were both confined, together, inside some sort of cramped, metallic lift that was rising sluggishly but smoothly, upwards, through a towering and slender shaft—a lofty framework of interlaced steel—that reached from top to bottom of the sunken salt cavern that plunged four hundred feet underground! Radiant bars of light irradiated every other squared section of the soaring structure. Where was the un–jolly giant taking him?

Hazard figured he'd be a goner for sure if he tried grabbing his gun. How to fight a mighty titan like that in such close quarters? Complete and utter disablement—and perhaps some surprise. No time to think about it! Just do it!

Dropping his legs down, impulsively, Hazard drew back both of his arms in a wide U–shaped arc, elbows bent, before letting both of his balled fists fly at the muscleman's crotch—both front and back! Unfazed, the muscleman slung Hazard across his hip to the floor—slamming him backwards into the base of the lift. Menacingly, the muscleman straddled him as Hazard, stunned, lifted up his frightened eyes to see that wrathful face staring down his nose with a grisly grin. Hazard cocked his knee and tried to thrust–kick his heel into the crotch of the muscleman, who caught the flying foot by the ankle with the Vise–Grip of both huge hands—twisting it, wrenchingly! Turned over onto his stomach, the muscleman thrust his own heel into Hazard's shoulder blades, knocking the wind out of him. Onward, that lift sluggishly crawled up that steeple–like shaft!

Stooping, the muscleman grasped Hazard by the nape of his neck, hauling him to his feet and slamming him face–first into the lift's metal wall. Hard—bloodying his mouth and nose! Whirled around, Hazard tried to knee the muscleman in the groin, reaching awkwardly for his gun in that waistband, but fumbling it. Uselessly, his Beretta clattered to the floor. Onward, that lift continued its sluggish climb upwards.

Stiff–arming him against the lift wall, the muscleman clutched at Hazard's throat, clenching it tightly as he literally lifted him off the floor to hold him up and strangle him to death with one huge hand! Desperate, Hazard balled up his fist, his middle knuckle protruding, and let a left–hook punch fly to the muscleman's temple! Unfazed! Choking, Hazard crunched up the thumb and fingers of his other hand, letting three palm–heel strikes of his right fist blindly fly in quick succession! Punching at the muscleman's eyes and nose, the nostrils spurted blood, the stranglehold faltering slightly. Flagging, Hazard forcefully rammed the heel of his palm underneath the muscleman's jaw, shoving it upwards with all his might—or what little there was left of it!

Grinding his teeth, and convulsed with rage, the infuriated muscleman hammered Hazard's head with his huge clenched fist, battering him straight to the floor—nearly knocking him senseless. Heaving, Hazard lolled on the floor, feeling immovable, paralyzed, done for. Mindlessly, his palms scrambled across the floor, making his eyes pop once one of his hands—breathtakingly, miraculously—brushed the grip of his dropped Beretta 70 pistol! He snapped it up and started firing blindly at the prodigious figure, blurred by his bleary eyesight, bending again, both arms outstretched, both huge hands grasping to tightly squeeze the neck to a hair's breadth! He fired all ten rounds in rapid succession until the magazine clicked empty!

At the top of the vertical, cavern–high elevator shaft, the lift's cramped compartment—in the shape of a silver, half–hexagon—bumped to a gentle stop. Its doors hissed open.

Backed into a corner of that compartment, Hazard still sat on the floor upright, his legs outstretched, his gun hand limp upon his lap. Before him, the bloody, bullet–riddled body of the hulking he–man lay sprawled in a lumpish and leaden heap.

§

A little later on, after retracing all of his lumbering, exhausted footsteps, Mark Hazard finally found his way back to the salt cave's entrance portal.

"My compliments, Gabriela!" he called out glibly to the pretty young girl as he passed by the reception desk heading out. "Your salt therapy's nothing if not—*exhilarating!*"

She looked aghast, disbelieving, as Hazard made his hasty exit, passing through the revolving glass–doors and trespassing upon the outside world—alive and well!

ELEVEN:

A
MEDIEVAL
ENCOUNTER

GREVGATAN
STOCKHOLM, SWEDEN

From one of those numerous brown folders, from one of those numerous piles of brown folders bearing the top–secret red star, Mark Hazard recalled, foreign nationals collaborating with the Islamic State network spanned several countries—including Australia, Belgium, Denmark, France, Germany, India, Netherlands, the United Kingdom—and Sweden. Incredibly, an estimated three hundred Swedish nationals, identified by either citizenship or residence permit, had travelled to join the ongoing civil war in Syria. **Castle Corsetry** had its satellite chapter in Stockholm as well.

Twin double–glass doors, each framed by eight mahogany squares, opened out from the rather nondescript, five–story brownstone building. From either side of that entrance jutted the pair of faintly flickering black lanterns. Inside, the lively corsetry fashion show was already in full swing.

It was a small, peach–carpeted stage sidled by a pair of twin potted green plants sprouting tall from their golden urns. Its pilasters and moldings were graven in gold. Its backdrop was a wide white projection screen. From behind tall, wine–colored drapes emerged each of the twelve comely and curvaceous corset models, strutting and swaggering their way across the stage, flaunting their well–favored, scantily–clad shapes to the reverberating, upbeat rhythms of some rackety, electronic music as they descended a short flight of steps to make their separate exits downstage.

Once more, Mark Hazard was privileged with a front–row seat, attended by the show's madame corset–maker, a pretty and petite young girl named Karin Lager, who dressed casually in her tight dark skirt and a gauzy, tan, V–cut top fastened by just a tiny, solitary button, accentuating her slender, hourglass figure. Her wavy, brown, shoulder–length hair was brushed straight back from her high, shiny forehead and sprightly eyes in a clip. Her rather long nose separated her high, rosy cheekbones. And her pretty full ruby lips drew back across her big sunny smile.

"As you see, Mr. Hazard," Karin Lager remarked wryly, referring to the dramatically different shapes, sizes, and styles of the universally lovely models parading across that stage, "there's no body fascism here—just a great enjoyment of the female form, both sexy and provocative, as well as fun and lighthearted—a true celebration of women's sensuality and frivolous glamour!"

"Hear, hear!" Hazard approved, applauding. "You certainly have a penchant for curves. I certainly have no prejudice against that!"

"We're *starving* for flattering female curves," Lager said gleefully, "pastel colors, silver, and gold that balance sinful designs with modern inspirations! I want to celebrate both the corsets and the optimistic ideas of the eighteenth century—the daring fashion of Marie Antoinette and the progressive ideas of Voltaire! I suppose I want to say thank you to all these heroic human rights fighters—that with their optimism and courage—have paved a way for a better world for us all to live in!"

"This collection certainly emphasizes all of that," Hazard agreed, looking askance at the girl, "not to mention plenty of femininity."

"For me," Lager said seriously, "corsetry is a very special sort of art—a jewelry that's dependent upon the collaboration between client and corsetmaker—as well as the ability to create a perfectly fitted garment according to actual physical specifications."

"I can appreciate that corsets are highly specialized garments having many uses," Hazard said suggestively.

"Indeed," Karin Lager nodded, looking askance at him. "They can be used for foundation under other dresses or act like shapewear. They can support the bustline and permit the use of strapless dresses overtop. They can cinch in the waist or smooth over the hips. Which particular specification were you most interested in?"

"I'll be perfectly frank," said Hazard, turning to address Karin Lager more directly, "I'm most interested—as are my principals at Transworld Corporation—in meeting with Gustaf Klein to urgently discuss his most specialized design."

"I see," Lager said, taken aback, pausing her prudish sipping from her sparkling champagne glass. "Meet me tonight at eight to discuss the details."

"Where?"

"At the *Den Gyldene Freden*—it's a restaurant in the *Gamla stan* section of Stockholm about nine minutes from here."

"I know it well," said Hazard, smiling familiarly. "I'll be there."

§

DEN GYLDENE FREDEN
GAMLA STAN
STOCKHOLM

Gamla stan, Stockholm's old town, is also known as *Staden mellan broarna*—the town between the bridges. It dates back to the 13th century and consists of medieval alleyways, cobbled streets, and archaic architecture. **Den gyldene freden** or the **Golden Peace**, an 18th century tavern located on Österlånggatan, is one of the world's oldest restaurants—having been in business continuously since 1722!—the longest–run restaurant with unchanged surroundings.

Hovering over its cobbled corner, the restaurant building rose four stories, its sandy brown facade punched by black–framed, rectangular windows. Its first floor was most decorative with windows, sidled by solid black shutters, having overgrown flower boxes; and its front entrance of double ebony doors with a tiled doorstep, all warmly aglow from the dimly flickering lantern that jutted from the wall above.

Inside, in one of the restaurant's various arched recesses, Mark Hazard sat at an ebony table overspread with a spotless white table cloth. It was dimly lit by a lone, faintly flickering candle. He had on a thick white silk shirt, dark blue trousers of Navy serge, dark blue socks, and sharply–polished black moccasin shoes.

He was partaking of the restaurant's famously delectable Swedish köttbullar, or meatballs, and brown cream sauce with mashed potatoes, broccoli, and tart and tangy lingonberry jam. Across from him sat Karin Lager with her remarkably flavorful meal of inlagd sill, or pickled herring, new potatoes, chives, and sour cream with strawberries for dessert. Hazard was drinking the highest grade brännvin vodka; she was drinking a Swedish punsch cocktail. They kept their conversation impeccably concise.

"I specialize in couture corset–making," Karin Lager boasted with unabashed pride, "and that means top quality corsets for women with high demands and a taste for beautiful eye–catchers—all made carefully by hand, all made to measure."

"Where are they made?"

"We make all our corsets in our ateliér," she told him. "Since the corset is never worked on by anyone else, we're able to offer our clients the ability to choose every single detail on their corset after discussing their ideas, combining their dreams with our knowledge of how to create the perfect shape."

"Combining dreams is precisely what we wish to discuss with the inventor of this extraordinary apparatus," he suggested.

"Everyone has different dreams, Mr. Hazard—different

ambitions and aspirations," she said skeptically. "How can we be certain that your vision compares and parallels with ours? It's a question of compatibility."

"Rest assured," Hazard said encouragingly, "even were they to ever differ, you can be absolutely certain that our dreams shall never oppose or compete with your own. We have absolutely no desire to appropriate the patent to your apparatus. My principals at Transworld Corporation propose only to invest in further refinement and perfection of the apparatus."

"In return for what?"

"Only its occasional employment for our purposes—for which we're prepared to pay quite handsomely, of course. That's why we feel it's critical to discuss terms directly."

"We're always curious about interesting collaborations," she said with an accommodating tone.

"Can we arrange a meeting then?"

"Tonight?"

"Would that be possible?"

"At our ateliér," Karin Lager told Hazard with an air of daunting finality, "at midnight."

§

Mårten Trotzigs Gränd
Gamla stan
Stockholm

It's the narrowest street in Stockholm, making the **Mårten Trotzigs Gränd** alley—once referred to as the Stairs Alley—a forbidding and eerie place for a midnight rendezvous. Its tapering, thirty–seven stony steps slope down steeply between tall, ocher–colored buildings to its most constricted point, where it squeezes to just thirty–five claustrophobic *inches* in width!

At the designated address, Mark Hazard set foot on the dank alleyway's lowest–level landing. A faintly flickering lantern jutted from the wall overhead, above a slender, black–framed door already ajar. *Will you walk into my parlour? said the Spider to the Fly!*

Instinctively, Hazard drew out the Beretta 70 pistol from beneath his armpit as he cautiously mounted the short flight of stairs that opened out to the roomy but dark and cramped studio space. Squinting, he ran his eyes over the room regardfully. Elegantly ornate panels of pale purple, draped with thistle curtains, lined the walls. Crystal chandeliers hung from the low ceiling. Arrayed in the rear of the room were the tailor's cluttered wooden worktables and benches. Its smooth flooring scuffed quietly underfoot. Like silent but spooky sentinels, several corset–sporting mannequins kept watch at strategic spots around the room—their shadowed silhouettes looming in the lurid gloom. In their midst sat another darksome figure whose somber silhouette suddenly budged perceptibly!

"Don't move, Mr. Hazard!" the mannish voice calmly commanded him. "You're quite covered."

A faint spot of light from the ceiling suddenly illuminated the burly figure of a man sitting stoically at the low–set, round–topped table. He was a tough–looking thug who sported a tight–fitting black cap and a khaki–colored parka. His shifty eyes, separated by a broken nose, were heavily bagged. Deep clefts etched his hard–looking cheeks. His upper lip and square jaw bristled with tufted stubble. And he squarely leveled at Hazard a Intratec TEC–9, the Swedish–made 9mm blowback–operated semi–automatic pistol! It was capable of firing ten to seventy–two rounds depending upon the magazine.

"Good evening," Hazard said coyly, conspicuously dangling his pistol by its trigger guard from his middle finger. "I'll just put this away if I may."

"You may do so," agreed the thug, nodding. "Sit down."

"It's been a long time since I've seen a TEC–9," Hazard confided as he slowly holstered his pistol and settled into the facing armchair. "You're not Gustaf Klein, I take it."

"You take it correctly."

"Who are you then?"

"That's not relevant."

"What is relevant?"

"Why you persist so stupidly with this corporate pretense of yours."

"My corporate standing is quite legitimate, I assure you."

"If you consider the British Secret Service to be a corporation," the thug scoffed. "What we want to know is how you tracked Gustaf Klein to Stockholm."

"Oh, that," said Hazard, smiling amiably. "A gloating Polish gentleman in Romania named Boczkowski referred me."

"That Boczkowski always was a babbler—the fool!" the thug remarked with scornful contempt.

"It's still in Mr. Klein's best interest to meet with us to discuss further research and development of his extraordinary device," Hazard insisted sincerely.

"It's in your best interest to start saying your prayers, Mr. Hazard," the thug told him forebodingly, "because you simply cannot be permitted to pester Mr. Klein. Your charade is at an end."

"Oh," Hazard desponded, looking suddenly downcast. "I was afraid you'd say something like that. Then I suppose I'll simply have to fall back on Plan B."

"What the hell's that?" exclaimed the thug, raising his gun to aim it at Hazard emphatically.

"It should arrive any moment now," Hazard said solicitously. "I should strongly advise you to put down your weapon and sit extremely still. Or else we'll both be very dead."

Just then, a clamorous commotion was suddenly occurring downstairs—a rackety disturbance that could be heard audibly by Hazard and the thug upstairs.

"Go! Go! Go! Go!" came the frenetic shouts of macho command.

And within seconds, Hazard and the thug were solidly surrounded, on all sides, by several stalwart and decked–out soliders who had violently kicked down the front door and, hustling and bustling noisily, hurried headlong up the stair-way to burst thunderously into the room!

Pointed toward Hazard and the thug, as the soldiers en-circled them even more closely, were the 17.7–inch barrels of their Swedish–made, Ak 5, 5.56mm gas–operated, rotating bolt automatic carbine assault rifles!

Openmouthed, the staggered thug promptly plunked down his weapon and, disbelieving, spread both of his sweaty palms flat upon the table top.

"Well, my dear roughshod friend," Hazard quipped play-fully with a simpering smile, "allow me to introduce you to the Swedish Security Service!"

TWELVE:

TODAY FOR ME, TOMORROW FOR YOU

JOSEPH COVINO JR

SKOGSKYRKOGÅRDEN
WOODLAND CEMETERY
GAMLA ENSKEDE
STOCKHOLM

Hedged round by a 2.4 mile–long limestone–granite wall, nestled on a ridge pervaded by dense groves of towering pine trees, the woodsy cemetery of firs and evergreens spreads expansively over 267 acres like an elongated rectangle. Inside its semi–circular main entrance, its rolling landscape, hills, meadows, and open spaces, all reach far and wide. In the distance, its lofty pine woodland crops up as a darksome green silhouette. From that entry point, a half mile–long processional path lined with thickset trees—known as the *Way of Seven Wells Path*—winds through the grassy woodland to the cemetery's southward section. Some ten thousand pine tree trunks, many dating over 200 years old, soar amongst 100,000 somber gravestones like mighty Roman pillars, their countless crowns forming a thick canopy set against the azure sky.

At that colonnaded entry, as well, a towering stone cross of darkened granite—known as the Holy Cross—shoots up sky–high from its grassy carpet; looking like a mighty giant welcoming visitors with wide open arms.

"Dr. Gustaf Klein," Hazard, stepping up to the lone, tallish figure of a man standing at its pedestal, ventured, "I presume?"

His close–cropped brown hair was brushed back to the left from his high, sloping forehead. His wide eyes, set beneath thin brows, were keenly intelligent and alive with intellectual fervor. His cheeks were sallow, his other features smallish—ears, nose, chin—his mouth's thin lips pursed by an impish smile.

"Welcome to Forest Cemetery, Mr. Hazard," Klein

131

greeted him, pressing his hand.

"Quite a curious place for a rendezvous, isn't it?"

"Not at all," he answered contrarily. "It's a beautiful oasis of perfect peace and tranquility."

"I see."

"This cross," Klein speculated, gesturing to the lofty relic, "could be seen as a symbol of faith—or, rather, as a symbol of the eternal cycle of life and death, darkness and light, joy and sorrow."

"Or," Hazard suggested, "it could be seen simply as a cross—or as solace."

"Just so," he acceded with a nod of accord, "it bears witness to the fragility of life. Shall we stroll as we talk?"

They tread a meandering path, lined with birches and conifers, that turned and twisted its way through a pastoral landscape, complete with a prodigious pond strewn with water lillies. Sunlight shimmered through the treetops, buzzing with skittishly chirping birds, and fluttered amongst the tombstones. With the scent of the pine trees mingled the smell of freshly cut grass. Headstones were small—a tangled mélange of wood, stone, glass, ceramics, and iron crosses, some sunken into the ground to their hilts; all arranged in dislocated blocks throughout the century–old pine forest.

"It's hard to believe," Klein recounted, "that all of this was once a gravel quarry—full of nothing but gravel pits. Now it's become an organic mystery that unfolds itself as you wander through it. Everything blends so harmoniously with its natural surroundings. It's an eminently serene resting place."

"That scarcely matters when you're no longer alive," Hazard remarked irritably.

"The great Swedish actress, Greta Garbo, is interred here, you know?" Klein related, abruptly switching the subject.

"No, I didn't know. But then, we're having this meeting to discuss you and your device—not Greta Garbo."

"Quite. How did you find me?"

"That man of yours, whom we captured in the Gamla stan, proved to be very garrulous—even effusive, I'd say."

"Yes, he always was the talkative type," Klein commented with a disgruntled tone. "And you're no doubt anxious to learn how I became involved in this project."

"The curiosity's just killing me, doctor," Hazard said cuttingly.

"During the Cold War," Klein recounted almost whimsically, "it would've simply been a matter of enlisting all the German guided missile experts the Russians failed to recruit—and paying for them to come over here and work on this...undertaking. Loyal Germans. Brilliant technicians. All comrades obediently awaiting their orders."

"Intriguing. But, of course, the Cold War is long since past."

Gustaf Klein abruptly paused, stopping in his tracks to face Hazard squarely.

"Now it's just a different war," he said, gravely serious, "with a different cause—with different warriors—but it's still an extremely contentious *state* of war all the same!"

"A war to which you're willing to contribute a remarkably destructive weapon."

"We all have our reasons for joining our respective causes, have we not?" spouted Klein with a dismissive wave of his hand. "Besides, my apparatus isn't a weapon as such—it's a weapon magnet that attracts and draws it toward its intended target."

"That's a rather hollow distinction."

"Yes, but it's a distinction full of its own very unique kinds of scientific and technical challenges!"

"Such as?"

"Things you mostly wouldn't understand," Klein condescended, "like controlling the missile's gyroscopic settings—its roll, pitch, and yaw—remotely via a radio beam."

"Sounds straightforward enough," commented Hazard.

"Its explanation is plenty straightforward," Klein conceded. "Its actual execution proves to be much more problematic."

"How so?"

"The effective range of the transmitter's signal is one of the greatest challenges of any functional homing device," he clarified.

"You will, of course, have to come in to be debriefed about all this," Hazard reminded him gently.

"That's another thing I wanted to talk to you about."

"I'm afraid," Hazard told him rather sternly, "that's not something really open to negotiation at this stage, doctor."

Finally, the two came to the foot of a slightly steep flight of stone steps rising uphill right ahead of them.

"This is the way to **Meditation Grove**," Klein elucidated, gesturing to the stairs, "The higher you go the shorter each step becomes—in hopes that you feel peaceful rather than tired once you get to the top."

"Why should we trudge to the top at all," Hazard asked dubiously with an impatient simper, "my dear doctor?"

"Skogskyrkogården was most meticulously planned," he pleaded, "to create a calm and soothing atmosphere—and to elicit certain feelings from its visitors. Kindly indulge me, Mr. Hazard. This could very well be my last chance to experience this luxury, as a free man, in the circumstances."

"Lead the way, doctor," Hazard relented with an accommodating gesture and smile and, together, they started to mount the sloping steps.

"This is an uplifting place of meditative calm," Klein announced, panting slightly, once they reached the elm–clustered hilltop known as *Almhojden*. "Here one may contemplate the meaning of life—or death."

"I can see that," said Hazard, glancing at his Rolex wristwatch, "but I'm afraid there's little time left for meditation just now."

"There's enough," Klein disagreed as Hazard regarded him curiously. "Skogskyrkogården is still a working cemetery, you know. Some two thousand funeral rites are performed here each year. This cemetery, you see, was carefully designed to make landscape and nature a perfect point of departure for the dear departed, so to say. I regret to say that it must be my own departure point as well."

"I would agree with you, doctor," Hazard said worriedly, "but I fear we could be speaking at cross purposes."

"It may also surprise you to know, Mr. Hazard," Klein told him, ignoring his remark, "that there's a part of this cemetery that's devoted even to *Muslim* graves!"

"Really?"

"Indeed," he affirmed. "You should also realize that the Islamist network is so far—reaching that it extends everywhere—even to your own homeland in the United Kingdom—even to your own country, Scotland!"

"Scotland?" Hazard asked, aghast.

"My dear Mr. Hazard," Klein said imperiously, "every great terroristic movement has its crusading *sponsor!* And the name of this venture's sponsor just happens to be Cormag McGregor!"

"Disavowing responsibility for not sponsoring terror, is that it?"

"I'm not a wicked man, Mr. Hazard, I should like you to believe that. I'm merely an inventor who's understandably proud of his scientific achievement."

"I've come to collect you, doctor, not judge you."

Threading their way through the lofty elmwoods, they finally came to a clearing overlooking the grassy, sloping hillside.

"My wife's buried in this cemetery, Mr. Hazard," Klein told him solemnly. "If, by chance, there's anything much left of me after all of this, I should like the bits and pieces to be buried close, next to her."

"That's a rather morbid thought, doctor, but something I daresay you won't be worried with for some time."

Out of a clear blue sky, the elegant, lightweight, twin-turboshaft engine, Swedish **AgustaWestland AW109** heli-copter loomed ahead—its four, fully articulated rotor blades whirling smoothly—hovering high over the hillside.

"Your VIP transport's arrived," Hazard announced light-heartedly.

"I won't be going with you, Mr. Hazard," Klein asserted adamantly.

"Not going's not an option, doctor," Hazard, eyes nar-rowed, admonished him.

"I'm very much afraid that it is, Mr. Hazard."

Deliberately, Klein unloosed the self–belt girdling his double–breasted but short, navy blue, gaberdine Trench coat with the wide lapels. He calmly undid the only one of its ten fastened, front buttons. Peeling back its storm flap, he laid open the several cylinders filled with plates of explosives and fragmentation jacket! It displayed shoulder straps and encased Klein's stomach. An explosive belt!

"I'm just about to detonate this suicide vest, Mr. Haz-ard," Klein announced sober–mindedly. "So, unless you care to be blown up along with me, I strongly suggest that you put about fifty feet between me and yourself—and pretty promptly, too! Right now!"

At one jump, his jaw dropped and eyes popped, Haz-ard turned on his heel, dashed, and dove headlong over the declining hillside. He only heard the thunderous blast, but never saw the uproarious explosion that obliterated Klein's body, shredding his torso and blowing it to bits—his cleanly severed head thrown completely clear of his shattered car-cass! Or, the helicopter abruptly scaling the heights of the sky at the shocking sight of the fiery, riotous blast!

All Hazard heard, just before the startling detonation,

was Klein's heart–stricken outcry shouted out in Latin:
Hodie mihi cras tibi!
Today for me, Tomorrow for you!

THIRTEEN:
ONE OF THE MCGREGOR CLAN

From one of those numerous brown folders, from one of those numerous piles of brown folders bearing the top–secret red star, Mark Hazard recalled, foreign nationals collaborating with the Islamic State network spanned several countries—including Australia, Belgium, Denmark, France, Germany, India, Netherlands, Sweden—and the **United Kingdom**. Incredibly, an estimated 400 British citizens had joined the Islamic State. If those who had joined had double citizenships, the government instituted a practice of stripping them of their British citizenship to prevent them from returning to the UK. By 2017, reportedly, 150 persons had been stripped of citizenship and were thus unable to re–enter the United Kingdom again. Now Scotland figured into this overall scenario—but how, specifically?

GARE LOCH
SCOTLAND

An open sea loch aligned north–south, **Gare Loch** is 6.2 miles long with a prevalent width of 0.93 mile. At its southern end it pours into the Firth of Clyde—the mouth of the River Clyde, Scotland's third–longest—through the Rhu narrows. Situated on Scotland's west coast, the river comprises the deepest coastal waters in the British Isles—538 feet at its deepest! On Gare Loch's western shore lies the village of Rosneath just north of Rosneath Point, giving the name Rosneath Peninsula to the whole body of land separating Gare Loch from Loch Long to the west. On Gare Loch's eastern shore lies the town of Helensburgh, the largest settlement on its banks. Other towns and villages bordering the loch include Argyll, Clynder, Garelochhead, Rhu, Rosneath, and Shandon.

In her wake, the 288–ton, **Mangusta 132E** luxury yacht left a frothy white trail as she sliced a smooth swath across the loch's placid surface. Her sleek, silver superstructure's

130–foot–8–inch hull surged ahead through the loch's murky waters at an easy cruising speed.

And she was flying the national flag of Scotland—or St. Andrew's Cross—with the argent X–shaped saltire defacing the blue field of blazoned azure!

Bringing up the rear of the yacht, like a bolt from the blue, an ebony, 8.7–foot–long, 551.3–pound **Kawasaki SX–R 160 Jet Ski** personal watercraft abruptly appeared— skimming across the waters, at breakneck speed, in hot pursuit! Its high–performance, 4–cylinder, DOHC, 4–stroke engine propelled it forward, full–tilt, in the yacht's foamy wake. Standing upright in the Jet Ski's rearmost foot tray was a lone, tall, and dark figure of a man, gripping tightly its handlebar controls. His rather cruel, ruthless, and water–smitten face betrayed a grimly unflinching expression. It was Mark Hazard, sporting swimwear, who was piloting that watercraft!

Cormag McGregor was a wealthy Scottish industrialist very much in the public eye. It was no great feat, then, for the Secret Service to locate him and put him under discreet surveillance. What was he doing cruising in Gare Loch in his luxury yacht—in such close proximity to **His Majesty's Naval Base, Clyde(HMNB Clyde)**, sited at Faslane on the Gare Loch, one of three operating bases in the United Kingdom for the Royal Navy. Most significantly, it's the navy's headquarters in Scotland as the home base for Great Britain's nuclear weapons, in particular, nuclear submarines armed with Trident missiles.

It was going to be a terribly risky but crafty gambit. But Hazard had to get aboard that yacht, somehow, and discover Cormag McGregor's intentions and whether he harbored any untoward designs.

Hazard's sleek jet ski shot past the cruising yacht as both craft buffeted the loch's gentle waves. Abruptly, but deliberately, Hazard cut across the boat's bow as he tore through the waters to precede the ship and forerun it! Then he weaved back and forth in front of the yacht, rather recklessly, tilting from side to side as his jet ski raced across the loch's calm surface! If that didn't attract their attention, nothing would!

Then it came time to play a little chicken with that yacht's unsuspecting occupants!

Hazard flew forward, right ahead of the yacht, going the round of the loch in one wide, sweeping arc until he turned abruptly about—steering his jet ski, full–tilt, directly toward the boat's oncoming bow! Only at the last conceivable second did Hazard swerve left, veering off on one side of the bow to avoid plowing into it—the water exploding in a spurting spray of sudsy spume!

Much to the presumed consternation of the yacht's doubt-less stupefied crew, Hazard wheeled around, doubling back on his jet ski to repeat his daring and impudent perform-ance! Bowling along, after going another round of the loch with another broad arc, Hazard hurtled headlong toward the bow of the oncoming yacht! At full speed, the yacht looming ahead, Hazard bore down upon the boat's bow—running his jet ski full tilt against it! Once more, only at the last conceiv-able second, did he swerve right, veering off on one side of the bow to avoid colliding with it!

Only this time, in his most madcap maneuver, Hazard abruptly applied the brakes and skidded deliberately into the side of the ship—screeching shrilly across her single-skin composite hull until he turbulently overturned, his jet ski capsized, its 3–blade, oval–edge stainless steel impeller protruding bottom upward! Stunned yet alert, Hazard was sprawled prone in the frigid loch waters, shivering, soaked, and praying for a prompt marine rescue!

Hazard never saw the 13–foot **Zodiac Yachtline 400** in-flatable boat, driven by its 50–horsepower Honda outboard engine, skim speedily across the loch surface, its PVC/ Strongan tube bobbing choppily up and down in the water to reach him. All he was conscious of were the two brawny crewmen who hauled him roughly into the boat to transport him to the idled yacht, carrying him aboard.

Before long, coming back to his senses, Hazard found himself sprawled supine on a spotless white twin bed inside of a maple–paneled cabin. A row of circles in the ceiling threw faint light upon his face as he lifted up his eyes. Venetian blinds hung over the cabin's single, sealed picture window. Above the bed's headboard, a stainless white set of cabinets projected slightly from the wall. On either side of the headboard stood a twin pair of ebony nightstands, each bearing a shiny, silver–metal, white–shaded lamp. One supported a decanter of water.

Sluggishly, Hazard got to his feet to take a peep through the blinds, hoping to catch a glimpse of the outside.

"So," the deep, guttural baritone voice unexpectedly interrupted the attempt, "you look none the worse for wear."

Hazard whirled around to cast his startled eyes on the tall, imposing man addressing him.

"I'm Cormag McGregor," he announced, bluntly introducing himself. "I'm the master of this vessel."

"I suppose I should say," Hazard stammered, hesitant, "permission to come aboard, sir?"

"Permission granted," came the harsh reply.

Cormag McGregor cut a striking figure even if he was a mostly balding man with a broad, shiny crown, his elongated ears fringed with bristling tufts of graying hair. His face was lean and hard, and deeply etched, his wide brown eyes deep–set beneath dark, bushy brows; his hollow cheeks dented with deep clefts. His full mouth, hinting at both brutality and sensuality, was fringed by a neatly trimmed, dark, and full but graying Vandyke beard that only emphasized most prominently his rock–solid chin. He was, indeed, the most regal looking man Hazard had ever set eyes on. He was decked out in tartan garments of woven wool and spoke in strong, r–rolling Scottish burrs!

"Well," Cormag McGregor commented coarsely, looking down his long, sturdy nose at Hazard, "I don't know if you're the most foolhardy person I've ever come across—or the most maniacal!"

"Probably a bit of both, sir."

"As it happens," he admonished him, "there are plenty of less precarious ways of making my acquaintance—Mister *Hazard!*"

"You've heard of me then?" Hazard asked, his eyes brightening.

"Your reputation has preceded you ever since the indelible impression you made on some of my Romanian friends."

"Oh," said Hazard, abashed, his head bowed down, his eyes upraised. "I see."

"Yes," Cormag McGregor sniggered, "*Oh!*"

"Well," he added hurriedly, "scrub yourself up and then join me in the lounge for a proper drink. We've much to discuss."

"Like why you've confiscated even my mobile phone," Hazard, patting his empty left armpit, suggested with a slight hint of contempt.

"My dear Mr. Hazard," Cormag McGregor condescended to him sternly, "you're to be my honored guest—albeit *un*invited—for several short days. During that time, you're to have absolutely no contact of any kind with the outside world. After that time, so long as you comport yourself peaceably, you'll be released, so to say—perfectly healthy and unscathed—to go your merry way."

"Most magnanimous of you."

"Quite," Cormag McGregor acceded with a nod, adding ominously. "Should you defy, resist, or otherwise oppose those simple terms in any respect, however, you shall be most unceremoniously, expeditiously, and effectively...*dematerialized!*"

Or as Yasin Salih might've put it, Hazard recalled grimly, he'd be compelled to go behind the sun—and simply disappear.

FOURTEEN:
SECEDING
FROM
THE
REALM

GARELOCHHEAD
GARE LOCH
SCOTLAND

Evenly aligned circles in the ceiling threw their faint light upon the yacht's spacious but soundless lounge and dining room areas, separated along one wall by a tall, gleaming, silver–surfaced ebony bar where Cormag McGregor was standing stoically, waiting for Hazard to come in. On either side of the roomy space, four broad, rectangular picture windows framed with maple looked out on the placid loch outside. Sitting on a window ledge, a lone, potted plant sprouted from a silver canister.

"You'll have a Scotch, of course!" McGregor stated flatly, more as a command than a question, once Mark Hazard did finally set foot on the space's plush carpet.

"The water of life," Hazard consented casually. "Of course."

"From which region?"

"Region?"

"My dear fellow," McGregor condescended with conspicuous pride, "there are as many brands of Scotch whisky as there are distinctive distilleries—and the regions—from which those originate. Being from Edinburgh, I prefer the single malts from the Lowlands for their lighter and grassier flavours. I still keep bottles of *Rosebank* from Camelon on the Forth and Clyde canal! And you?"

"Well," Hazard deliberated, "my father being from Glencoe, I suppose I'll settle for a single malt from the Highlands."

"Excellent!" McGregor approved. "As it happens, I have a bottle of *Loch Lomond* single malt—thirty–year–old—perfect for the occasion!

"Occasion?"

"Our mutual venture!"

"I'm not with you."

"You will be."

Presently, Cormag McGregor served their respective drinks in shiny, four–and–one–half–inch tall, lead–free crystal *Glencairn* whisky glasses!

"That's twenty–seven *drams*—precisely!" McGregor boasted.

"Perfect," Hazard complimented him, taking his glass. "Thank you."

Atop a maple pedestal, placed in a recess of the room, rested a sculptured bust of **Sir William Wallace**, the cele-brated Scottish knight and national hero who gained honour by leading the First War of Scottish Independence!

"*Scots, who have with Wallace bled,*" Cormag McGregor recited from the patriotic song of Scotland, **Scots Wha Hae**, written by iconic poet, Robert Burns, after observing Haz-ard taking notice of it. "*Scots, whom Bruce has often led, Wel-come to your gory bed, Or to victory.*"

"It's also the party song of the Scottish National Party," McGregor added, "of which I'm a proud supporter!"

Hazard sniffed gently at the drink's aroma before sipping it, nodding and smiling pleasurably.

"*Lay the proud usurpers low,*" Hazard recited the song's concluding lyrics. "*Tyrants fall in every foe, Liberty's in every blow, Let us do or die.*"

"Good!" McGregor heartily approved, gesturing to the buoyant, oyster–white, U–shaped sofa overspread with black, gray, orange, and white throw–pillows. "Sit down!"

For a moment, Hazard felt like he was back in Lon-don being ordered around the room by EM—the Executive Minister of the Secret Service!

Between them was placed a broad, low–set maple coffee table.

"Do you love your country, Mr. Hazard?" McGregor asked abruptly, plunking himself down across from him.

Taken aback, Hazard hesitated, reflecting reluctantly.

"I'm just a humble servant of the Crown," he answered, faltering.

"The Crown!" McGregor raised his voice in contemptuous protest. "Don't be coy, man! Do you love *Scotland?*"

"She's part of the Realm," Hazard said non–committally, "I have to love her."

"The Realm!" McGregor glowered with scornful disdain. "How far would you go to protect Scotland?"

"Protect her, sir? From whom?"

"Don't be dense, man! *From* the Realm?"

"Does Scotland require protection from the Realm?"

"You decide," McGregor told Hazard, getting to his feet and waving at him to follow. "Let's go up on deck."

Hazard followed on McGregor's heels as he led the way through the dining area, past an oblong, maple–topped dining table girdled by six ebony chairs, to a narrow, winding staircase that meandered upwards to an open–air deck above. There was a twin pair of facing, bracket–shaped, oyster–white sofas, overspread with several cobalt blue and white throw–pillows, separated by an upright, white–topped maple bar lined with four tall white stools.

McGregor gestured for Hazard to sit down on one or the other of the two molded plastic chairs with cobalt cushions that were placed before the frontward sofa, facing foreward.

"I've anchored here at Garelochhead to prove my point," he related seriously.

"What point's that, sir?"

"**Garelochhead Training Camp** is located here," he recounted, "eighty–two hundred acres, complete with gun, grenade, and mortar ranges—not to mention two parachute drop zones—where up to five hundred British military personnel can play their little war games!"

"And?"

"The **Royal Naval Armaments Depot**," McGregor continued, holding up a halting hand, "based at the village of Coulport on Loch Long, is the storage and loading facility for the nuclear warheads of the UK's Trident programme. That's just 6.2 miles from Garelochhead—ten minutes away. RNAD is linked with the **Defence Munitions Glen Douglas** military munitions depot, likewise located near Loch Long."

"So, there's a decided military presence in the area," Hazard deadpanned.

"You're being infuriatingly coy again, Mr. Hazard," McGregor growled.

"It's unintentional, I assure you. I just don't see what you're driving at."

"Even closer," McGregor related testily, "is His Majesty's Naval Base, Clyde, which is sited at Faslane on the Gare Loch. It's just 1.6 miles from Garelochhead—where we are now—and just two miles east of RNAD Coulport. It's the Royal Navy's headquarters in Scotland and home to Great Britain's nuclear weapons—in the form of nuclear submarines armed with Trident missiles. Garelochhead's the nearest town to the HMNB Clyde naval base."

"Would any of this, by chance, explain your presence in the area?"

"What I'm driving at is this, my friend," McGregor said pointedly, "Scotland's 5.3 million citizens represent about eight percent of the total UK population. And those nuclear submarine and Trident storage bases are located just twenty miles from where two–fifths of the entire Scottish population lives! Scotland doesn't want those damned things there!"

"Where would you relocate them to if you could?"

"I'd stick them next door to the Houses of Parliament!"

"Hardly practical," Hazard jeered with a grin.

"Point is," McGregor clarified, "removing Trident nuclear missiles from Scottish waters would reduce the capability of the British armed forces to wage its wasteful wars abroad.

For far too long, far too much of Scotland's vast energy resources have been uselessly squandered by corrupt Westminster politicians on their costly foreign military adventures!"

"North Sea oil reserves, you mean?"

"Precisely."

"What's the program then, Mr. McGregor?"

"It's about nuclear weapons, Mr. Hazard!" he growled again. "It's about peace! It's a hugely important thing to thousands and thousands of people all across Scotland!"

"Peace, you say?"

"It's public knowledge that I support the Scottish National Party," McGregor expounded, "which advocates for a nuclear–free Scotland that becomes a sovereign state completely independent of the United Kingdom! The party is unequivocal in its strident opposition to nuclear weapons—and the stationing of the UK nuclear deterrent at the Faslane naval base in particular. Scottish independence would result in the removal of nuclear weapons from this country!"

"I'm no geo–political expert," Hazard conceded, "but if Scotland became independent, it would paralyze the nuclear defensive stance of the UK for years. It would also blow a huge hole into NATO's defensive posture at a time when that alliance is being tested unlike anytime since the end of the Cold War. As the entire nuclear submarine infrastructure that the UK depends on is based in Scotland, relocating it would be hugely expensive and time–consuming."

"None of which is disagreeable to Scotland—or undesirable."

"I sympathize with your sentiments, sir," Hazard commiserated, "but given the sluggish pace of Westminster politics, I don't see what you envision happening anytime soon."

"Perhaps there's a way of forcing Westminster's hand," Cormag McGregor suggested forebodingly.

"Perhaps that wouldn't be exactly...*proper.*"

"What's propriety got to do with it?" McGregor snapped.

"All I'm interested in is what's fair and just for Scotland, nothing else."

"Just now, however," he added hurriedly, "I have some other important matters to attend to. I heartily recommend you to go aft to take advantage of the outdoor amenity at the stern of the ship."

"I'll do that. Thank you."

Cormag McGregor turned on his heel and they promptly parted company.

Hazard readily found his way to the spacious afterdeck that was furnished with another bracket–shaped, oyster–white sofa overspread with the standard white and cobalt blue throw–pillows. Behind the cushioned sofa stood another tall, white, maple–topped bar lined with four tall, white stools.

That amenity, Cormag McGregor mentioned, was a roomy, rectangular, acrylic hot tub bath, braced by a frame structure and hedged round by a cedar ledge, and boiling over with frothy and steamy water. Emerging from the spa, just then, was the most extraordinary and startling sight!

Out of that fuming bath, bubbling up with creamy foam that clung to her beautiful body, climbed the tall and lithe young girl with the satiny, sunburnt skin, her delicate hands grasping the arched bars of the stainless steel rails as she heaved herself upwards, mounting the short spa steps. Her pale beige scraps of bikini made her look stark naked!

She looked absolutely stunning! Hazard couldn't believe his dazzled eyes as he stood in awe of her, breathless and aghast.

She was the comely Moroccan girl Hazard had trysted with at the Villa Mandel in Transylvania in Romania: *Zara!*

FIFTEEN:
A NON– CONJUGAL ENGAGEMENT

Nonchalantly, Mark Hazard sat down and sank back into the downy sofa, his arms outstretched along the tops of the cushions. Zara, standing before him in all her half–naked, eye–filling glory, drenched and dripping, snapped up a fleecy towel to wrap herself with, squeezing the ample mounds of her supple breasts pleasingly upwards.

"Well," Hazard asked her quizzically, "what in hell are you doing here?"

"I belong here!" she answered, petulant. "What's your excuse?"

"I'm on a job."

"I'm on a mission."

"I gathered that already. Only, I strongly advise you to terminate that mission forthwith—whatever it is."

"Why should I do that?"

"Because it'll be my job to ruin your mission."

"The odds of you succeeding at that, Mr. Hazard," she hissed, "are, I'm afraid, heavily against you."

"Really?"

"Really."

"Does your host know about our...*conjugation*?"

"Don't be ridiculous. If he did, I'd be dead."

Hazard grunted doubtfully as he got abruptly to his feet, raising his chin rearward. Grudgingly, she turned around to set her eyes on the most unsettling sight.

Just then, the speeding, armoured, 48.8–foot, 22–ton Island–class patrol vessel—a ballistically protected police patrol boat operated by the **Ministry of Defence Police** and propelled by twin caterpillar C18 engines—slowed down to come alongside abaft the yacht. The Island–class is a class of police patrol boat operated primarily by the MOD Police Clyde Marine Unit at HMNB Clyde. They are tasked with protecting high value Royal Navy ships such as the Vanguard–class submarines.

The MDP is a civilian special police force which is part of the United Kingdom's Ministry of Defence, whose primary responsibilities are to provide armed security and counter terrorism services to designated high–risk areas, as well as uniformed policing and limited investigative services to Ministry of Defence property, personnel, and installations throughout the United Kingdom. Their marine support units are responsible for the waterborne security of His Majesty's Dockyards and HM Naval Bases—this one, in particular, based at HMNB Clyde. The 43 Commando Fleet Protection Group Royal Marines, part of 3 Commando Brigade, operate those boats.

That police patrol boat boasted a crew of just three— sporting the black polo–type shirts and trousers with black jackets—two of whom emerged decked out in ballistic body armour and black Kevlar helmets. They each adroitly brandished the **Colt Canada C8SFW**, gas–operated, rotating bolt assault rifle with the 20–inch barrel that fired the 5.56×45mm NATO cartridge.

"What in hell's all this in aid of?" Cormag McGregor, emerging from the lounge entry behind the bar together with his two brawny crewmen, spouted irately. Zara slid guardedly in back of the bar herself.

"You really didn't think that I'd come aboard without my marine support group waiting in the wings," Hazard asked him, simpering haughtily, "did you?"

"No," McGregor relented with a knowing smirk, "I suppose not. What next?"

"Nothing," Hazard said flatly, "except that I'll have my gun and phone returned promptly—unless, of course, you care to have this extravagant tub of yours thoroughly searched from stem to stern."

"My dear fellow," McGregor condescended, "we've done nothing criminal or illegal. We're guilty of nothing except performing a rescue at sea. And you've been accorded nothing but the most courteous and gracious hospitality!"

"Rescue scarcely warrants confiscation—my property if you please."

"With pleasure," McGregor readily acceded, turning to one of his brawny crewmen. "Retrieve Mr. Hazard's...*paraphernalia.*"

"Much obliged," said Hazard.

"So," McGregor proposed, "I suppose you'll be departing with your rather over–dressed friends?"

"Not at all," Hazard demurred. "You promised to take me on a pleasure cruise for several days, remember? And I'm holding you to it. In fact—"

Betrayed by her heavy bell of golden hair, ablaze in the sunlight, none other than Mary Goodknight emerged unexpectedly from the police boat cabin! She was dressed in a black–and–white cotton shirt tucked into a wide hand–stitched black leather belt above a medium length skirt in shocking pink. She climbed aboard the yacht's stern platform and hastily mounted the short flight of six arched, maple steps rising to the deck's railed, stainless steel gate.

"Oh, Mark!" she cried. "I saw your accident from ashore and called for help right away! I hope I did the right thing!"

"As always, my darling," Hazard complimented her, laying his hands on hers, having a firm hold of the rail, "you did the most impeccably correct thing!"

"And who's this very lovely lass?" asked Cormag McGregor, stepping up to greet them as he handed over Hazard's gun and mobile phone, which he took with a nod of gratitude. He casually holstered the one and pocketed the other.

"This is Mary," Hazard told him by way of introduction. "She's my *fiancé.*"

"We're engaged to be married!" Goodknight chimed in excitedly. "Isn't it wonderful?"

"Marvellous," McGregor said dubiously, "my compliments to you both."

"Felix is flying in tomorrow to help with all the arrange-ments!" she chirped. "He's being such an absolute dear about everything!"

"Felix?" McGregor interjected.

"He's our best man," Hazard said in a staid tone. "Nei-ther of us has any relations to speak of. So he's our major witness as well."

"Ah," sighed McGregor. "I see. Well, Miss Mary—"

"Goodknight, Mary Goodknight."

"Well, Miss Goodknight," McGregor bid her invitingly, "perhaps you'd care to stay overnight aboard the yacht."

"Oh," Goodknight demurred, "thank you, but no. Hon-estly, I think I ought to go. I should get back to meet Felix in Glasgow. Mainly, I just wanted to make sure Mark was all right."

"Nonsense!" McGregor exclaimed. "Mark is perfectly healthy as you can see! I insist that you accept the hospitality of my yacht for at least one night. We have a small crew of only six in three cabins. Our other five cabins can accom-modate up to eleven guests so there's plenty of room. It will give us all a chance to become better acquainted after our shared...*experience!*"

"As you're engaged," McGregor added somewhat sternly, "no conjugal visits shall be allowed aboard ship. So you may bunk with our other lovely lady in residence—Zara."

Mary Goodknight glanced around to run her appraising eyes over the becoming young Moroccan girl, smiling scru-pulously, once McGregor nodded toward her. She was still swabbing her shapely body absentmindedly with her towel.

"I'd like a quiet word with my fiancé," Hazard spoke up.

"Might I suggest the fore deck," said McGregor, gestur-ing to the lounge entry nearby. "There's a comfortable and private spot there. Permit me first to buy your good lady the best drink on Gare Loch!"

Ever gallant, Hazard relented as he watched Mary

Goodknight follow on McGregor's heels as they stepped inside the lounge. With a thumbs–up gesture of gratitude, and an appreciative smile, Hazard dismissed the expectant MOD crew with a friendly wave of his hand; the police patrol boat directly sped off.

"Fiancé?" Zara asked daringly, laying a firm hold on Hazard's arm. "Does she know about our...*conjugation*?"

"Don't be ridiculous," Hazard simpered. "If she did, I'd be dead!"

§

Later on, at the bow of the boat, Mark Hazard sat together with Mary Goodknight on the forward sundeck, relaxing on another of the yacht's bracket–shaped, oyster–white sofas opposite another twin pair of facing molded plastic chairs with cobalt cushions. In front of them stood a round, maple–topped table bearing their chilled drinks. Beyond, a twin set of dual, cobalt blue, frontward–facing wedge pillows with white cushions were set aslant for unstrained sunbathing.

"Your target's Zara," Hazard told Mary Goodknight urgently, taking both of her hands in his and clasping them tightly upon his lap. "You'll have to search her belongings thoroughly."

"What am I looking for?"

"An extraordinary woman's corset—as exotic as she is."

"Corset? And once I've found it?"

"Take pictures of it—front and back—and send them to Felix straightaway."

"How will I recognize the correct corset in case there's more than one?"

"You can't mistake it. Its boning is loaded with transparent microelectronics."

"Then what do I do?"

"You wait to substitute an imitation corset for it—a duplicate look–alike."

"Where will I get that?" Goodknight asked, incredulous.

"That's the trickiest part," Hazard conceded. "Felix is standing by at a safe house in Glasgow—where he's in possession of the full line of corsets by the creative corset–maker, known as Gustaf Klein, whose complete collection was confiscated from a laboratory in Stockholm. Hopefully there's an identical corset in Klein's wardrobe—preferably neutralized—to change for the original."

"If not?"

"If not," Hazard said gravely, "this entire operation will have to be aborted in favor of resorting to more direct and drastic measures."

"Assuming that I put the replacement in its place," Goodknight asked curiously, "how will I dispose of the original?"

"That's the easy bit—you simply put it on and wear it off the yacht."

"What's Zara supposed to be doing whilst I'm rummaging through her things?"

"Preferably she'll be asleep after you've slipped her a mickey finn," Hazard said, sliding a gold–and–platinum ring—having a sizable prong setting—from his little finger and, changing hands, switching it to Goodknight's left ring finger. "Your engagement ring. Its gemstone cap contains a potent dose of **chloral hydrate**—so don't waste it. Put it into her drink and she'll be out for the night."

"How pretty!" Goodknight said as she held out her hand to the sunlight to inspect the sparkling ring. "How will I ever receive the replacement to substitute for the original in such a short time?"

"Time's of the essence, my darling Goodknight," Mark Hazard acknowledged with an ironical smile. "When it absolutely, positively *has* to be there overnight, relax…it's *Federal Express!*"

SIXTEEN:
ALL
IN
A
NIGHT'S
WORK

For the first and last time, Mary Goodknight and Mark Hazard were introduced at dinner to the yacht's six–man crew, consisting of the first mate, the engineer, the chef—and, of course, those two brawny, omnipresent marines. For the occasion, Hazard had been spared a battered black–and–white dogtooth suit, dark blue Sea Island cotton shirt, and black silk knitted tie.

"I'm the captain!" Cormag McGregor bragged with swagger. "He's the mate and there are two for the engine room and pantry. We don't call it the mess deck aboard this yacht. All Scots!"

McGregor promptly dismissed both the first mate, Fletcher, and the engineer, Stewart, to perform their various duties.

"The mate's standing a 4–8 watch on the bridge," he related. "The engineer's monitoring the engine room, naturally."

Those two laconic marines, Morrison and Murray, standing in their respective corners, were each packing holstered sidearms—specifically **Glock** polymer–framed, short recoil–operated, locked–breech semi–automatic pistols. In their cases, Hazard observed, the **Glock 26**—the 9×19mm sub–compact variant designed for concealed carry.

As for McGregor's pantry chef, Macpherson, he came and went, dutifully serving the sumptuous feast of Scottish cuisine, including: **partan bree**, a seafood soup with crab and rice; **cabbie claw**, young cod soused in white sauce with chopped egg whites; **kedgeree**, smoked haddock, flaked, with boiled rice, parsley, hard–boiled eggs, curry powder, and cream; **rumbledethumps**, a vegetable dish of potato, cabbage and onion; and for dessert, burnt **Trinity cream**, a rich custard base topped with a layer of hardened caramelized sugar flavoured with vanilla. They sealed the meal, so to say, with **Drambuie**, a golden–coloured, 40% ABV liqueur made from Scotch whisky, heather honey, herbs and spices.

It was a quiet and uneventful dinner—until, that is, Zara, who'd been explained away rather enigmatically as an honored guest from her native land of Morocco being taken on a grand tour of several of the standing freshwater lochs in the vicinity—strictly a pleasure cruise—suggested that she and Mary Goodknight retire to their cabin with some ginger wine for some serious "girl talk."

From the bar, Zara brazenly snapped up a couple of stemmed glasses together with a full bottle of **Stone's** ginger wine, a fortified wine made from a fermented blend of ginger, raisins, sugar, yeast, and brandy.

"Ginger's been proven to be an aphrodisiac," she remarked suggestively, "which could prove useful in discussing Mary's impending nuptials with handsome and dashing Mark here!"

Hazard hung his head, hiding his reddened face, wondering, worriedly, whether Zara would let something revealing slip and give them both away! She didn't.

"Splendid idea!" Cormag McGregor complimented her approvingly. "A true heart–to–heart talk between two admirable—and very virtuous—ladies! Carry on!"

In passing, Mary Goodknight embraced Hazard briefly but warmly in his chair, kissing him modestly on his cheek before the two girls quit the dining room for their cabin.

"Goodnight, darling!" Hazard said endearingly, laying hold of one of Mary Goodknight's forearms and kissing it softly before she left.

Without a word, Hazard got to his feet and directly went out, making his way to the yacht's open–air sundeck at the boat's bow, taking his Scotch whisky glass with him.

"Watch him!" Cormag McGregor, rising to follow Hazard, paused to order his two brawny marines. "Closely!"

§

Triple rows of circles in the ceiling threw their faint light upon Zara's compact cabin, which was furnished with a pair of spotless white twin beds with matching, fleecy white pillows. Separating the beds, at their headboards, was a glossy black nightstand with twin maple drawers. Atop the nightstand rested a brightly glaring, black–stemmed, white–shaded lamp. Along one wall stretched a lengthy white storage cupboard. Along the other wall hung the white venetian blinds draping the lengthy picture window overlooking the placid loch outside.

They'd plunked down their red–and–gold labeled bottle of **Stone's** ginger wine and two glasses atop the nightstand. In such close quarters, it was no difficult feat for Mary Goodknight to drug Zara's glass with the powdery, rapidly dissolving **chloral hydrate** from her *faux* engagement ring, whilst Zara was changing clothes, putting on her gossamer nightgown. Before long, the drug took its stupefying effect.

"I feel faint," Zara complained, turning pale as she sprawled supine upon her bed, her head lolling against her pillow.

"Take it easy," Mary Goodknight said, bending her knee to comfort her, gently caressing her furrowed brow. "You probably had a little too much to drink."

"Mixing liqueur with wine was a bad idea," Zara murmured, her breath erratic.

Mary Goodknight was sorely tempted to interrogate the drugged girl but her priority orders were clear: find a certain corset, photograph it, and promptly disseminate it. A couple of strictly feminine questions couldn't hurt in any case.

"I have a feeling you've met Mark before," Mary Goodknight whispered suggestively in Zara's ear.

"What makes you think that?" Zara asked, her lips slackening.

"Woman's intuition. How well do you know him?"

"Intimately," she mumbled with a knowing smile.

"Zara," Mary Goodknight pressed her, "why are you really here?"

"I must meet another man…a Commodore…"

"A Commodore? Where?"

"I must escort…"

"What's this Commodore's name?"

"I must…"

"His name, Zara, his name!" Mary Goodknight rasped.

"I cannot tell…," Zara stammered as she blacked out, deeply unconscious, sinking into undivided oblivion.

"The devil take you!" Mary Goodknight cursed frustratedly, getting abruptly to her feet.

Making doubly sure the cabin door was locked, she proceeded to ransack Zara's studded closet wardrobe until she found it. Mark Hazard was right—it was unmistakable!

Mary Goodknight spread the support garment across her own bed as Zara lay insensible on hers. It was an elegant green–and–gold **Evanna** corset—18th century–inspired—of beautifully patterned woven cotton brocade with metallic inserts. She painstakingly photographed it—front and back—and duly communicated it to Felix Lighter via her mobile phone.

Returning the corset to Zara's closet, for the moment, Mary Goodknight sat down on her bed, her hands fidgeting nervously in her lap as she anxiously awaited some response. Then she cast her eyes on Zara, so peacefully reposed, and carefully and thoughtfully contemplated the surpassing youthful beauty of her face and form, brooding upon both.

§

Night was falling with the setting sun. Flat waves rippled gently across the loch's surface, reflecting the low–lying hills sprawled across the faraway horizon, suffused with layered hues of phosphorescent, purplish yellow.

"Have you everything you need?" asked Cormag Mc-Gregor, still playing the gracious host, as he stepped up quietly to the sundeck where Mark Hazard was reclined at length against one of those spongy, cobalt blue wedge–pillows. "You don't mind sleeping out here?"

"I enjoy it," answered Hazard. "I prefer this fresh air to that canned air–conditioning inside. And it's rather marvellous having all those stars to look at."

"It's a starless sky, Mr. Hazard," McGregor differed. "Besides, I wouldn't take you to be the star–gazing type."

"It just goes to show how little you can know people."

"I know you well enough to know you like playing cat–and–mouse games," McGregor countered. "Only I assure you, you will discover absolutely nothing illicit taking place aboard this yacht."

"Nothing terroristic, you mean?" Hazard suggested challengingly.

"You should take care, Mr. Hazard," McGregor admonished him ominously. "There could be a certain passenger who inadvertently fell overboard and who, unhappily, got caught in the propellers once we came about to attempt a search and rescue. How sad. So tragic a mishap. And just as we were all becoming so very fond of him."

"I seriously doubt that should occur, Mr. McGregor. You know full well you're being very closely surveilled by now."

"You're probably quite right, my friend," McGregor conceded with a whimsical wave of his hand, "but it is a delectable thought nevertheless."

"Depending on your point of view, I suppose."

"Your point of view has become rather murky by this time, I daresay."

"I suspect you're right about that. There's nothing more for me to see here. I should probably depart with my betrothed tomorrow."

"All things considered, a well–advised decision."

Hazard caught a surreptitious glimpse of his mobile phone which just received a silent text message from Mary Goodknight that declared, and displayed, simply:

Ready to take delivery.

It was time to create a small–time diversion.

"Till then," Hazard slurred a little drunkenly, "we might as well amuse ourselves and have some fun."

Far beyond his outstretched feet, well out of reach, Hazard had already placed upon the sundeck his strategically planted whisky glass. He promptly drew out his Beretta pistol from his armpit, took careful aim, and fired—shooting and shattering the glass to pieces!

Cormag McGregor abruptly held up a halting hand once his two brawny and ubiquitous marines came running, their glocks drawn! They stopped dead in their tracks.

"Really, Mr. Hazard," McGregor remarked wearily, "I expected something far less childish from you by way of antics!"

Holstering his pistol, Hazard lifted up his eyes with a shrug of his shoulders, looking as guileless as he could.

"Just something to discourage the idea of anybody trying to make me the man overboard," he suggested innocently.

§

Astern, Mary Goodknight was already crouched on the level, low–lying maple platform at the aftmost part of the yacht, waiting with bated breath.

Before long, a shiny steel hook, glinting in the moonlight, suddenly emerged from the lurid, rippling loch waters and punched the platform to take hold of it. It was firmly affixed to the right arm of Felix Lighter, who emerged along with it, sporting a complete black frogman suit and scuba set! He promptly handed over to her a transparent, watertight package containing the corset identical to the one photographed and disseminated!

"Special delivery!" Felix Lighter whispered whimsically, grimacing as he mouthed the words through his diving regulator. "Courtesy of the CIA!"

And with that, Felix Lighter promptly re–submerged and disappeared in a darksome, effervescent swirl of murky water and boiling bubbles!

SEVENTEEN:
AN
ASTUTELY
CLASSY
SUBMARINE

Cormag McGregor's luxury motor yacht was as-warm with energetic members of the 550–man unit of the 43 Commando Fleet Protection Group Royal Marines(43 Cdo FP Gp RM), part of 3 Commando Brigade, searching every nook and cranny of the craft, high and low, for Mary Goodknight, who'd mysteriously disappeared sometime during the night. They were carrying the gas–operated, rotating bolt Colt Canada C8 carbine assault rifle, that fired the 5.56×45mm NATO cartridge, and meant business as they stalked throughout the entire ship, prying into every hole and corner.

"Here," their captain ordered gruffly, "come on! Look round everywhere! Come on! Get cracking!"

"Where is she?" Mark Hazard confronted McGregor, standing astern, arms akimbo, once more.

"I've absolutely no idea," he equivocated. "She could be anywhere. She's probably someplace ashore."

"How every convenient," Hazard remarked resentfully, "to say nothing of inconceivable."

"My guests aboard this yacht are not prisoners, Mr. Hazard," McGregor said, mightily indignant. "They're free to come and go as they please!"

"When they're not taken hostage, you mean."

"That accusation is outright outrageous—as is this invasive and coercive search!"

"This vessel's arrested in rem," Felix Lighter, attending Hazard, interjected. "You'll be strictly prohibited from getting under way until further notice."

"My dear fellow," McGregor condescended coolly with a mocking smile, "we've absolutely no desire to set sail. We're perfectly content, in fact, to remain here indefinitely—for the time being."

Felix Lighter grunted doubtfully, beckoning Hazard with a sideways tilt of his head.

"It's high past time we paid a visit to the Naval Base

Commander, Clyde," Lighter said seriously once he took Hazard aside.

§

Henry Higham, Naval Base Commander, Clyde, also known as the Commodore, Clyde Submarine Base, was a surprisingly soft–spoken, boyish looking man with fine features, close–cropped but graying hair and a hearty, ruddy complexion. His high forehead was deeply wrinkled from constantly furrowing his brow. He sported a starched white shirt with a thin black tie. His shirt bore the commodore's 1.7–inch wide band insignia shoulder board and half–inch wide sleeve lace.

"After my bit of diversionary gunplay," Mark Hazard related to him, "the last message I received from Miss Goodknight indicated that she had successfully exchanged the garments, as planned, and that she was wearing the one containing the active apparatus."

"This young Moroccan woman you mentioned, named Zara, wearing the inactive apparatus?" Commander Higham offered.

"Whom Mary reported was obliged to meet a certain commodore."

"A commodore whom you speculate could be a member of the chain of command here at Clyde—including *myself* as a potential suspect."

"By virtue of sheer proximity, yes, though we have no information about any commodore's possible level of involvement."

"Besides myself, gentlemen, there are nearly *thirty* commodores attached to this naval base."

"She needs to contact only one," Felix Lighter, sitting next to Hazard across from the commodore's desk, interjected. "That's why we're keeping the yacht she's on under the closest possible surveillance to try and discover which commodore it could be."

"This is all so utterly unbelievable!" Commodore Higham exclaimed. "If this woman does indeed harbor some devious design, then what would be the purpose of ingratiating herself with one of our commodores?"

"Again, a matter of proximity," Lighter explained. "From a similar case we're already aware of, the purpose would be to gain access—most likely to the base itself."

"It's just too fantastic to believe," remarked Commodore Higham, shaking his head.

"Which begs the question, sir," Lighter persisted, "are there any unusual or extraordinary events, or happenings, scheduled to occur at Clyde in the near future? Impending, I mean."

"There is one, indeed, about to happen," the commodore confirmed. "Most imminent. It takes place tomorrow."

"What is it in God's name?" Hazard asked.

"The launch of our newest Astute–class nuclear–powered fleet submarine—HMS Agamemnon S123—and the test firing of her Tomahawk IV land–attack missiles! It's a demonstration and shakedown operation."

"Good God!" Hazard said with a start.

"Can you tell us a bit about this Astute sub?" Lighter asked.

"Astute's the most capable nuclear attack submarine ever built," the commodore boasted proudly. "She's Britain's deadliest nuclear asset. She's the Royal Navy's killing machine! Astute subs have stowage for thirty–eight weapons! Her nuclear reactor has a twenty–five–year lifespan before re–fueling's necessary. So she can circumnavigate the globe without surfacing. *We come unseen*, is our motto."

"We're playing this all wrong," Lighter admitted worriedly, turning to address Hazard directly. "We've got to release McGregor's yacht immediately so he'll show his hand!"

§

His Majesty's Naval Base, Clyde

HMNB Clyde, a Level One Nuclear Security site, is tucked away snug on the upper eastern shore of Gare Loch in Argyll and Bute, to the north of the Firth of Clyde and twenty–five miles west of Glasgow, the bay at Faslane converted into a marshalling yard to service the needs of the ships and submarines stationed there. Gare Loch is a sheltered sea loch on Scotland's west coast that opens out onto the River Clyde. Secluded and secure, Faslane sprawls alongside the deep and navigable waters of Gare Loch, providing ships and submarines swift and stealthy access through the North Channel out to the submarine patrolling areas in the North Atlantic and beyond.

§

Commodore Ephraim Hockley, one of Faslane's numerous office holders, was out to show off his gleaming, brand–new **Raptor CS230**, 230–brake horsepower, sports car with its baby blue, tubular chassis. He was out to show off, likewise, his comely Moroccan passenger—a carnal young girl named Zara—seated next to him in the black race seat of the car's open–air cage with the metallic blue, anti–roll bar. Shifting through the car's 8–speed gearbox, he bowled along the base's various lanes and byways until arriving at the naval command centre, pulling up to park.

No sooner did the commodore and his blithesome female friend fall out of the car were they both approached, and surrounded, by several stalwart, armed, and uniformed men sporting black polo–type shirts, trousers with black jackets, and police baseball caps. As sidearms, they were packing Glock 17 polymer–framed, short recoil–operated, locked–breech, semi–automatic pistols!

178

They gave the fetching girl's lengthy, beautified kaftan tunic, trimmed in gold and silver sateen threads, and heel-less, soft–leather slippers, or **balgha**, of dyed yellow, a quick once–over.

"Commodore Hockley?" the officer–in–charge addressed him.

"Yes?" answered the commodore, his mirthful smile suddenly turning sullen.

"My name's Vallings," the officer announced neutrally, "Ministry of Defence Police."

"What is this?" demanded Commodore Hockley, conspicuously perturbed.

But the officer, a rather beefy fellow, ruddy–complexioned, with kindly eyes, cherubic cheeks and a knobby nose, stayed stoical.

"Might we have a quiet word?" he asked simply but smiling manneredly.

§

NORTH CHANNEL

Displacing some 7400 long tons, surfaced, the HMS *Agamemnon*(S123)—the Royal Navy's Astute–class nuclear–powered fleet submarine—glided ponderously through the strait stretched between north–eastern Northern Ireland and south–western Scotland. She was named after the legendary king of Mycenae who commanded the Greeks during the Trojan War. Her bearing kept a north–west course toward the Atlantic Ocean for which she was bound. Her sleek, black, 318–foot–3–inch hull scythed through the rippling, wind–whipped waters—a frothy stream, churning and billowing at her sides, heaving a squally sigh as she surged onward.

And she was making imminent preparations to fire off and launch a Tomahawk Block IV cruise missile!

EIGHTEEN:
PROTECTOR
OF
THE
REALM

HMS AGAMEMNON(S123)
NORTH CHANNEL

Propelled by her Rolls–Royce PWR 2 reactor and 800 horsepower diesel generators, this Astute-class submarine could operate at depths of just about 1280 feet and traverse the waters at speeds of 29 to 30 knots whilst fully submerged. For all that dynamic power and might, her cursory Central Command voices gave their orders in remarkably matter–of–fact tones!

A monotonous alarm resounded shrilly three times.

"Action stations! Action stations!"

To the diving officer the commanding officer issued his command:

"X.O. Captain! Dive the submarine!"

"Dive submarine, Aye!"

"Diving now! Diving now!"

In a stormy swirl of convulsively churning waters, the submarine was swallowed whole, fully engulfed as she vanished from view.

To the control room the diving officer issued his command:

"Open all main vents."

Commands were expeditiously exchanged in preparation for missile launch:

"Instrumentation. This is command. Tube one is released."

"Weapon system in condition. Tube one for launch. Command, roger."

"Final T–zero prediction is valid. Command, roger."

"Command. All launch prerequisites have been met."

"SP concurs. Command, roger."

"Open tube. Stand by TLAM engagement."

"Supervisor. Initiate fire. One."

"Initiate fire. One. Denote one."

"Command. You have permission to fire."
"T–minus one minute and counting."
"Ten seconds."
"Five. Four. Three. Two. One."
"Launch!"
"Missile away!"

§

Mark Hazard and Felix Lighter were being smitten, their grimacing faces splashed and pelted by whipped up wind and water. They were being ferried across Gare Lock at top speed by a rigid inflatable boat, or RIB—that lightweight, high–performance, high–capacity boat constructed with a rigid, glass–reinforced plastic hull bottom joined to side-forming, partitioned air tubes inflated with high–pressure air, giving the sides resilient rigidity along the boat's topsides. Its rubberized fabric bottom is stiffened with flat boards within the collar, forming the boat's deck or floor. Its inflated collar acts as a life jacket, ensuring that the boat retains its buoyancy even if it's taking on water. Its design is stable, light, swift, and seaworthy. And its tough polyurethane tubes render it virtually knife–proof and bulletproof!

Aslant in the water, the 28–foot–long black boat, propelled by a roaring 300–horsepower outboard motor, was tearing across the Firth of Clyde—the mouth of the River Clyde—in hot pursuit of Cormag McGregor's luxury motor yacht! She was being expertly piloted by a member of the **Ministry of Defence Police** marine unit! At about thirty knots, even though the yacht was picking up speed, the two boats were about evenly matched. Over the howling din of the blustering wind and water, Hazard and Lighter shouted at each other at the top of their voices!

"That's sub's set sail and she's all set to test–fire that missile!" Lighter bellowed. "Mary's in the gravest danger! We've got to get her off that yacht and pronto!"

184

"What makes you think she's on board?"

"*Has* to be! She never came off! Hidden in some secret compartment! It's the only answer!"

"What about backup?"

"We're on our own, my friend!" Lighter affirmed, shaking his head. "No reinforcements! MDP won't act on suspicion!"

"Will we make it in time?" Hazard pondered aloud.

"That's the question!" Lighter yelled, pointing toward the oncoming yacht looming right ahead. "Ask *them!*"

Hazard directed his eyes to the yacht and promptly spotted Cormag McGregor's pair of brawny marines, each sliding hurriedly along the yacht's facing bridge wings—those narrow planked walkways extending outward from either side of the yacht and stretching from stem to stern.

Approaching rapidly from astern, her bow rebounding in the choppy waters, the MDP pilot veered the boat to port to cleverly give his pair of passengers—and their starboard shooting arms—their straightest and most direct line of fire!

Drawing near the stern of the yacht, the two marines were already reaching at their waistbands for their Glock pistols! Positioned in their shock–mitigating suspension seats, their rigid seat pans supported by airsprings and topped with upholstered foam cushions, Hazard and Lighter were already firing off their pistols, repeatedly—their shooting arms stiffly outstretched, rigidly braced, and taking deadly aim! McGregor's marines leveled their pistols at the inflatable boat, flying full–tilt, returning fire! Fiery sparks flew as zinging bullets ricocheted off the structural seat frames—far too close for comfort!

Firing first, and unswervingly straight, Felix Lighter's Walther PPK found its mark—hitting the marine treading the port walkway and sending him flying into the brimming loch! Luckily, Hazard's Beretta barely grazed the left shoulder of the marine treading the starboard walkway—just as

185

the target had leapt onto the yacht's stern platform, taking cover behind the upright bar!

By that time, Hazard and Lighter sprang from their seats and, as their barreling inflatable boat maneuvered closely to the stern of the yacht, overtaking it, they both dove headlong for the selfsame platform! Tumbling down alongside the elongated hot tub, they both abruptly sprang up, firing their pistols repeatedly at the bar's topmost surface—splintering it with bullets!

"I surrender!" crowed the wounded marine, slouched behind the bar, clutching at his bloodied shoulder.

Rashly, Hazard pounced upon the marine, kicking aside his discarded Glock pistol, wresting him to his feet by the scruff of his neck, slinging him bodily onto the sofa set in front of the bar!

"Where's the girl?" Hazard demanded as he and Lighter plunked themselves down on either side of the jittery marine.

Grimacing and groaning aloud, the marine shook his head adamantly.

"Listen, fool!" Lighter growled, "this tub could be blown to bits by a submarine missile any second now! Where's the girl?"

Again, another stubborn shake of the marine's head.

Abruptly, the crotch of the marine's trousers was ripped apart and left in tatters! Lighter held up his right–handed hook, flashing its glinting steel directly in front of the marine's face!

"I hope you've got a quickly curable itch, my friend!" Lighter threatened him menacingly. "By the time I'm through scratching it with this, you'll be singing with the Vienna Boys' Choir!"

For emphasis, grinding his teeth, Lighter sharply prodded the marine's groin with his hook's spiked point!

"Where's the girl?"

Adamantly, the marine nodded.

"Show us! Now!"

Wrested to his feet once more, the harrowed marine staggered through the yacht's nearby lounge entry, leading the way to a vertical bulkhead, directly adjacent to the lounge's upright bar, protruding flush with the wall. It was blocked out by four broad gray panels trimmed in black.

Once the marine threw the secret switch, the four panels slid smoothly aside as a whole hatchway, exposing to view the cramped soundproof sanctum consisting simply of a padded, oyster–white armchair set in front of a narrow, black, kneehole desk—atop of which was ornamentally placed a ceramic tea set, teapot, teacup, and saucer included, not to mention a gnawed–on apple!

Slouched in the armchair was Mary Goodknight, chloroformed and unharmed, but sluggishly coming to.

"Good boy!" Lighter complimented the marine mockingly, hauling him out to the stern platform, where he snapped up a nylon–coated, foam life jacket, slapping it against his chest.

"Abandon ship, mate!" Lighter ordered the marine lightheartedly. "I wasn't bluffing about that missile!"

Unceremoniously, Lighter shoved him overboard—the beleaguered marine clutching unsteadily at the life jacket as he plummeted into the loch with a jarring splash!

"Strip, Mary!" Hazard exhorted Goodknight as he roughly peeled off her cream–coloured Shantung silk shirt and charcoal, cotton–and–wool skirt. "This is no time for modesty!"

Then Hazard proceeded to uncoif that accursed corset! She staggered groggily. Her fleshy bosom cleaved deeply in her spare bra.

"Get her off this boat, Felix!" Hazard exhorted Lighter, hustling her into his receptive arms.

"Get us all off this boat!" Lighter countered.

"I've got something to do!"

"Not what I'm thinking!"

"Go, Felix, Go!"

Jostling them through the lounge entry, Hazard ushered Goodknight and Lighter to the brink of the yacht's stern platform.

"Don't wait for me!" he exhorted Lighter at the last. "Get her on that inflatable boat! Go!"

Hazard, after goading them both overboard, whirled around.

"Looking for me?" came the confrontational question from the frighteningly familiar and guttural voice.

Standing tall before him, unexpectedly, Cormag McGregor loomed large at the lounge entry!

"You've got to get off this boat with me!" Hazard exhorted him.

"You're no Scotsman!" McGregor challenged him irately through his tightly gritted teeth—ignoring the entreaty.

"I'm no terrorist!" Hazard countered.

"Hypocrite! You're an assassin!"

"Defender of the realm!"

"*Lackey!*" McGregor spouted, laughing aloud. "Whom I'm going to *kill* with my bare hands!"

McGregor flung himself at Hazard, lunging at him with both arms sturdily outstretched, hands clutching graspingly at his throat!

§

Tracking of the **HMS Agamemnon's** propelled Tomahawk missile continued cursorily:

"Glasses receiving telemetry."

"Telemetry looks good."

"Missile is on trajectory."

"There will not be a second T–zero. Command, roger."

"Missile is *off* trajectory!"

"Repeat!"

"Missile is *off* trajectory!

§

McGregor's crushing, vise–like grip held fast to Hazard's throat, throttling it. Hazard drove both of his hands upwards, palms pressed tightly together, spreading a wedge–block between his attacker's arms. McGregor rushed forward. Hazard, widening his hands, grasped McGregor's arms and drove a knee into McGregor's groin. Together, they both stumbled and fell into the seething hot tub!

Hazard turned, struggling to climb out. Tenaciously, McGregor laid a firm hold on Hazard's neck, clenching it tightly from behind.

"You're going down with this ship!" McGregor, enraged, growled angrily.

Choking, Hazard spun, plowing a sword hand into McGregor's groin, his strike slackened by the water. Useless! Hazard spun again, slamming a desperate roundhouse punch into the side of McGregor's head—making him recoil. It was just enough to escape McGregor's strangulating grip! Hazard awkwardly mounted the brim of the hot tub and jumped—diving headlong into the loch!

Like Lighter and Goodknight, he was promptly plucked out of the water by the MDP officer piloting the trailing, inflatable boat!

§

Drenched and dripping, McGregor clambered from the hot tub and staggered through the entry and into the yacht's lounge. Agape, all he caught sight of, fleetingly—before the missile struck—was the chic corset, pulsating throughout with its scintillating, rainbowlike colors, left wrapped round the sculptured bust of Sir William Wallace!

Exploding, the missile set the entire yacht ablaze in a fiery, yellow inferno that convulsed violently, and repeated-

189

ly, churning with raging black and orange clouds of earth–
scorching smoke!

EPILOGUE: *LOVING LEAVE OF ABSENCE*

MONA DAM RESERVOIR
KINGSTON, JAMAICA

Mark Hazard and Mary Goodknight sauntered leisurely together, arm in arm, along the sandy footpath that sidled the reservoir's narrow roadway. They were making the round of the 1.6–mile loop that encircled some 700 million gallons of dull blue water, spreading far and wide before them, reflecting the clusters of darksome clouds hovering aloft. Across the reservoir, a long way off, the somber Long Mountain bulged from the facing shore. They were gradually ambling toward the northeastern section of their circuit—once more.

"Now," Hazard quipped happily, full of play, "where were we before we were so *rudely* interrupted?"

"We were discussing domestic duties and household chores like cooking and sewing," she answered, just as sprightly, "as I recall."

"And possibly resigning from this disagreeable trade of ours."

"I can't imagine you ever resigning from the Service—not until the mandatory retirement age of forty–five, anyway."

"Perhaps you ought to look to the future more yourself, my darling Mary."

"How do you mean?"

"My last secretary was a beautiful bird," Hazard began to explain but added hastily, "though not nearly as beautiful as you!"

"Watch it, buster. Make your point."

"After five years with the service," he recounted, guardedly mincing his words, "she'd become a touch...*severe*."

"Understandable—given the pressures and responsibilities of the job."

"There comes a point, though, where marrying a career,

193

instead of a man, can turn one into a spinster."

"I'm in danger of becoming an old maid now, am I?"

"It was the agents in danger in the field whom she worried herself to death about, and she revered us equally, but she never had any intention of becoming romantically involved with any man who could be dead the next week."

"Am I romantically involved with anyone?" she asked coyly.

"Truth be told," Hazard brooded, avoiding answering her question, "appointment to the Secret Service is more of a form of *servitude*. For a woman, there isn't much left of her for other relationships. Any affair outside of the service automatically makes her a security risk, so she's left with only one choice: either resign, and lead a normal life, or resign herself to interminable servitude to King and Country."

"What has this rather depressing parable to do with me?"

"She'd started showing signs of stress and strain. She'd reached the time for decision when all her impulses told her to get out—even though the everyday melodrama of her quixotic world made it harder and harder for her to betray her proxy father by resignation."

"I hope there's a happy ending to this little fable."

"There is indeed," Hazard said matter–of–factly. "She left the Service finally to marry a dull but worthy and wealthy member of the maritime industry."

"What about you?" she asked him mindfully. "Why have you never married?"

"I expect because I gather I can handle life better on my own," he reflected. "Most marriages tend to depreciate rather than improve the people in them."

"You could have something there. But it depends on what you want to amount to. Someone contented or dissatisfied—and regretful. You'll always be incomplete by yourself."

"Well," Hazard said with a dismissive shrug. "I'm nearly married already. To a gent. Has the designation EM. I'd have to divorce him before I ever married a lady. And I'm not sure I'd care to do that. She'd probably come with all kinds of requirements and complications. I'd panic and flee to Japan or someplace like that."

"What about children?"

"I wouldn't mind having a few. But only after I retire. Not fair to them otherwise. This job's rather...*insecure*."

"You can get in a rut in any line of work. But I can see becoming fed up with being on your own, sooner or later," she ruminated rather morosely. "I suppose every girl would like to come home and find another pair of shoes in the foyer. Trouble is, I've never found the right sort of bloke to fit the shoes much less wear them."

"You sound like Cinderella in reverse," Hazard teased with a slight chuckle.

"What kind of woman might you marry then?" she asked him pointedly.

"Well," Hazard mused, examining Mary Goodknight minutely. "She'd have to possess all the finer qualities—be fair of face, bright, poised, witty, have a delectable figure, and like making love a lot."

"*Really*," she condescended, looking down her blushing nose at him.

"All the normal things," he added with a suggestive smile, "you know."

"Yes," she said cynically, "I'm afraid I *do* know!"

Just then, out of the clear blue sky, the black, lightweight, twin–engine **AgustaWestland AW109** helicopter—its turboshaft powerplants driving its fully articulated four–blade rotor system—loomed ahead, decelerating as it descended to slowly lower its elegantly designed fuselage until it hovered over a spacious expanse of grass. There it pitched slightly, its rotor arms swinging languidly, and settled with a light bump.

The pair watched with wonder, warmly embraced, grimacing against the swirling dirt and sand blown up by the machine's blaring engine. They stood, speechless, as the cabin's door flew open and a tall, lanky figure in gray alighted to the ground. He was a strangely familiar man with strangely familiar features and a strangely familiar gait, wearing a heavy–duty, double–breasted, gabardine Trench coat right out of the Cold War era! Leisurely, he moved toward them, both of his hands tucked deeply into his unbuttoned pockets.

Slowly stepping to the fore, Hazard positioned Mary Goodknight protectively under his arm as the stranger drew near.

"Oh, no!" she cried crossly. "Not again! Not now! Not so soon!"

"What's it now?" Hazard confronted the stranger as he came at them, sounding similarly cross.

"Lighter," he introduced himself, grinning but gesturing reticently to the helicopter, "CIA. Your luggage, passports, and various visas are all aboard. Your VIP air shuttle is all ready to ferry you to the airport and most deferentially awaits your pleasure!"

"Mark," Mary Goodknight, looking electrified, exclaimed, "what in hell's he on about?"

"Oh," Mark Hazard told her in a primly patronizing tone, "didn't I mention it? I've decided to take you on a long overdue and well–earned holiday—just the two of us—anyplace in the whole wide world your pretty little heart desires!"

Mary Goodknight's powerfully amorous eyes instantly welled out with tears—involuntarily, uncontrollably—as she threw her arms round Mark Hazard's neck, clinging tight, kissing him long, hard, and full on the mouth like no girl had ever kissed him before!

POSTSCRIPT:
ACCEPT NO SUBSTITUTES, THE REAL JAMES BOND

C arlisle, Pennsylvania—a borough and the county seat of Cumberland County situated within the Cumberland Valley, a richly productive agricultural region—is a far cry from being an exotic or glamourous locale for a James Bond novel! Carlisle was, however, the location where, during the summer of 1967, a tall and lanky kid of just thirteen, hand–printed on faded loose–leaf paper his 26–chapter, 119–page James Bond story! Its manuscript survives to this day. That was fifty–five years ago! And the kid, Yours Truly, is today 68—soon to turn 69 in a few short months!

At that time, I hailed from Pensacola, the westernmost city in the northwest Florida panhandle, in Escambia County, on the so–called Emerald Gulf Coast. I was visiting relations on the Pennsylvania Dutch–"white trailer trash" side of my mother's family. I was, in fact, staying at a Carlisle trailer park owned and operated by my maternal grandmother and her husband, my mother's step–father. I was left to live there for some weeks by my own mother after she returned to Florida with her second husband.

During that period, inexplicably, something possessed— and prompted—me to write my own James Bond story— perhaps as a way of passing the time during those long and wearisome summer days parched by the area's hot and humid continental climate. My collaborator–in–composition was my maternal aunt, Lynne—a shapely and sultry brunette babe who'd married my mother's brother, Herbert. She was a stay–at–home trailer housewife who was also an avid reader of mass paperback novels! When I got stuck on some creative problem, impeding the story's plotting, Aunt Lynne would cannily suggest some clever and plausible scenario to help me progress smoothly with the story's various transitions.

At that point in time, of course, America, and indeed the whole wide world, was in the tenacious grip—throes, really—of *Bondmania*, a global phenomenon! Even as a budding teenager, I was no less fanatic, and fervent, in my preoccupation—obsession even—with all things James Bond!

My fixation with James Bond was, of course, directly due to the imposing film performance of **Sir Sean Connery**, who cut such a striking figure as the first, original, and still best big–screen, cinematic incarnation of the fictional British Secret Service agent in the spy flick by Eon Productions, **Dr. No**(1962)—its worldwide debut occurring in Great Britain 60 years ago on the 5th of October. **From Russia With Love**(1963)—yes, still the best and most Fleming–faithful of the film series—premiered in London, right away, roughly a year later on the 10th of October. Shortly after, this pair of superior Bond films started screening as popular and profitable double–bills at cinemas all across the land. Before long, as well, I was carrying around my own plastic playtoy replica of Bond's trick attaché case—complete with its stinky, cap–exploding booby–trap!

Every woman wanted him, every man wanted to *be* him! was a popular catchphrase of the day. Or every male teenager as well, maybe. I labored under no illusions about ever *being* James Bond 007 aka Sir Sean Connery, no matter how strongly I was tempted to attempt to emulate either. After watching the major motion pictures I was inspired, in turn, to read the original source material for the films: the twelve remarkably creative novels and two short story collections written by **Ian Lancaster Fleming**(28 May 1908–12 August 1964)!

Five years following the debut of **Dr. No,** whilst stuck in Carlisle, Pennsylvania, I was powerfully inspired—somehow—to try my hand at writing my own James Bond tale, more a hodgepodge of the movies than anything from the novels. Long since, though, I've read through very mindfully—from cover–to–cover with the most meticulous care, not to mention multiple times—each and every last James Bond novel and short story! To this very day, in fact, I keep in my possession the original tattered and crumbling paperback copies of the novels first published in the 1950s and 1960s! And I consult those regularly for reference. As a result, my dear readers, I *know* James Bond! As, indeed, my current James Bond–like novel—**World Without Want**—shall duly attest to anyone else who really and truly *knows* James Bond! Which, in itself—some fifty–five years after the fact—clearly brings my own writing career full circle!

As an aside, my dearly beloved father, **Joseph Sr.**, to whom this novel you're holding is so fondly dedicated, dearly adored James Bond aka Sir Sean Connery! So much so that I can clearly recall exact moments in the films when he conspicuously reacted to the on–screen action—as when, in **Dr. No**, Connery as Bond throws bear–hugging Puss Feller, aka Lester Pendergast, into switchblade–wielding Quarrel, aka John Kitzmiller, during their barroom fracas; or as when, in **Goldfinger**, M, aka Bernard Lee, dresses down Bond for his temporary incompetence, admonishing him if he fails to shape up: *"This isn't a personal vendetta, 007. It's an assignment, like any other. And if you can't treat it as such, coldly and objectively, 008 can replace you."* Because circumstances separated us by the time I entered the fourth grade in 1964, sadly, we watched only the first three Connery flicks together.

Because I do know the admirable James Bond of the books so well, and remain so closely acquainted with him, I become rather infuriated at times with how the **Eon Productions** films have so inaccurately misconceived the character, or deliberately distorted him outright. With the ruinous onset of the hyper–pretentious and artificially contrived quackery of political correctness, even any remote semblance of the true James Bond character was essentially killed off with the ill–advised commencement of the utterly fatuous era of Pierce Brosnan's male–model portrayal of Bond! By the dawn of Daniel Craig's charmless, humorless, and thuggish portrayal, Bond's deplorable demise was altogether complete. James **Bland**, indeed!

Both Brosnan's and Craig's portrayals remain remarkable solely for being so utterly **un**charismatic!

And, incidentally, James Bond of the books has never, ever been so stiffly self–conscious—as mis–portrayed in the movies so stupidly—about either ordering vodka martinis "shaken–not–stirred," or delivering his supposed "signature–line" of self–introduction: **Bond, James Bond!** Where those concerns did occur, they took place naturally, simply, and unpretentiously as embodied by a very reserved and unassuming James Bond.

Far worse than the cinematic distortions of the literary James Bond are the deliberately revisionist perversions unfairly, and dogmatically, inflicted upon the character by countless, self–superior, contemporary commentators peddling to the public at large their supposedly learned and enlightened, but wholly warped politically correct outlook. These misguided, hack commentators are the ones who resort to their misinformed name–calling to mis–characterize James Bond as racist, misogynist, sexist—and every other conceivable "*ist*" mis–label in the book!

For any "*ist*" label to properly apply, incidentally, some existing sense, or attitude, of superiority must present itself. And James Bond of the books acts superior to nobody, as a rule, except perhaps the bad guys—the villains—and rightly so! Why these witless commentators persist with attempting to impose upon the character their shallow and superficial labels is way beyond any and all rational comprehension!

Of course, you could engage in endless kamikaze, schoolroom debates, or dissertate infinite treatises, relating to these profoundly debatable subjects of Bondian controversy! But why waste the time or effort? So long as you persist with mis–representing the character, whatever your pretext or excuse, you'll remain woefully **WRONG!**

Take, per prime example, a couple of excerpted phrases from a recent book review(26 May 2022)of Anthony Horowitz's third continuation James Bond novel, *With a Mind to Kill*, by–lined by one Gwendolyn Smith, who refers falsely to Ian Fleming's *"careless treatment of women,"* calling the original novels *"sexist"* and *"nonsensical."*

Nonsensical, quite the contrary, are these half–witted hacks, peddling their comatose politically correct doctrines, who've so obviously never, ever read the first word of Ian Fleming's brilliant and supremely creative James Bond novels!

Over the course of those books, James Bond's bacon is saved, or otherwise preserved, numerous times by several *"strong"* women:

•In **Moonraker**(1955), it's Special Branch agent, Gala Brand, who most meticulously instructs Bond how to re–set the gyroscopic course of the Drax missile targeted to destroy London!

•In **Diamonds Are Forever**(1956), it's Tiffany Case who helps a badly battered and beaten–up Bond to escape murderous gangsters from **Spectreville** on a railroad handcar!

•In **Thunderball**(1961), it's Domino who, during a death struggle underwater, saves Bond from strangulation at the deadly hands of Largo by shooting the villain through the neck with a spear–gun!

•In **You Only Live Twice**(1964), it's Kissy Suzuki who rescues Bond at sea and prevents him from drowning, following his hundred–foot plunge from a helium balloon, during an arduous half–mile swim!

•**From A View To A Kill**(1961), the short story, it's assistant Mary Ann Russell, during another death struggle at a forest, who saves Bond from a killer by shooting the assailant with a .22 target pistol—even whilst four special forces–style soldiers remain afraid to fire for fear of hitting Bond!

Point being: if you presume to comment on the James

Bond novels so **DUMBLY** then at least take the time and trouble to actually **READ** the bloody books first!

When it comes to women, at worst, James Bond of the books is slightly chauvinist if overtly protective of them. He doesn't hate women any more than they hate him. He's no misogynist, sexist, or any other sort of artificially concocted "*ist.*" And contrary to the movie misrepresentations, he's no libertine, promiscuously sleeping around and going to bed with multiple women, either; with rare exception, he involves himself intimately with one—and only one—woman per novel. A mightily sensitive soul, he consistently treats his women with the utmost gentility and respect.

And another thing: these artificially mannered and supposedly "*feminist*" females populating the more modern and supposedly enlightened movies do **NOT** constitute "*strong*" women, either! True inner **strength** of **character** comes from **within**, it doesn't emerge from without. Grimacing, glaring, scowling doesn't make you "*strong,*" ladies, any more than perennially **whining** about what a victim of **"sexism"** that you are! Nor does spouting rude, obnoxious and petty put–downs of Bond, either. That proves, simply, how shallow and superficial of a personality you are—nothing more.

Something else the movie–makers can duly dispense with, speaking of women, are those ridiculously silly "sex scenes" in which the players frantically paw at one another, ripping and tearing their clothes off, whilst swapping spit and tongues with all the delicacy and finesse of a rabid pair of slobbering, lip–smacking camels–in–heat! It's neither erotic nor sexy. It's just plain, cringingly *BORING!* James Bond of the books makes carnal love to women with a languid elegance and grace—not with the ungainly clumsiness of some awkward, inexperienced school boy!

As for the future, pressing forward, James Bond is, has been, and always and ever shall be half Scottish–half Swiss. And no matter whatever the witlessly unthinking movie–

makers, or brain–dead hack commentators, might attempt to artificially contrive: James Bond, like it or not, is neither black, nor gay, nor a girl, nor anything else except a warm–blooded, unapologetically Caucasian, straight, heterosexual, and marvellously male British subject and civil servant!

Period!

Bond's deep reflections in Goldfinger(1959)say it all so read it, my dear Johnny–come–lately revisionists, and weep: *"Bond came to the conclusion that Tilly Masterton was one of those girls whose hormones had got mixed up. He knew the type well and thought they and their male counterparts were a direct consequence of giving votes to women and 'sex equality.' As a result of fifty years of emancipation, feminine qualities were dying out or being transferred to the males. Pansies of both sexes were everywhere, not yet completely homosexual, but confused, not knowing what they were. The result was a herd of unhappy sexual misfits—barren and full of frustrations, the women wanting to dominate and the men to be nannied. He was sorry for them, but he had no time for them."*

There's a mouthful that should dishevel many a bushy man–bun!

This novel was thus lovingly written—with undivided reverence and veneration—to rightly honour and pay unabashedly proud tribute to that incomparable legacy!

Accept no substitutes!

LONG LIVE THE REAL JAMES BOND!

WORLD WITHOUT WANT

WORLD WITHOUT WANT

JOSEPH COVINO JR

WORLD WITHOUT WANT